Murder in the Pleasure Gardens

MURDER
in the PLEASURE
GARDENS

ROSEMARY STEVENS

BERKLEY PRIME CRIME, NEW YORK

MURDER IN THE PLEASURE GARDENS

A Berkley Prime Crime Book
Published by The Berkley Publishing Group,
a division of Penguin Group (USA) Inc.,
375 Hudson Street, New York, New York 10014.

First edition: May 2003

Library of Congress Cataloging-in-Publication Data

Stevens, Rosemary.
    Murder in the Pleasure Gardens / Rosemary Stevens.— 1st ed.
        p. cm.
    ISBN 0-425-19051-X
    1. Brummell, Beau, 1778–1840—Fiction.   2. Great Britain—History—George III, 1760–1820—Fiction.   3. Courts and courtiers—Fiction.   4. Dandies—Fiction.   I. Title.

PS3569.T4524 M8 2003
813'.54—dc21

                                                    2002038472

PRINTED IN THE UNITED STATES OF AMERICA

10   9   8   7   6   5   4   3   2   1

This book is dedicated with many thanks
to Johanna Hoffman

Acknowledgments

For their much needed support and encouragement, I wish to thank Barbara Metzger and Connie Koslow.

Special thanks goes to my friend Melissa Lynn Jones for her assistance in researching Regency social customs and language. Any errors in the story are, of course, my own.

Finally, for his love and understanding while I was writing this book, I want to thank my son, Tom Stevens. You are simply the best!

❧ Author's Note ❧

Besides Beau Brummell, the other real historical personages in this book are: George, Prince of Wales (later George IV); his Royal Highness, Frederick, the Duke of York; her Royal Highness, Frederica, the Duchess of York; Charles, Lord Petersham; Earl Spencer; Lord Headfort; John Lavender; James Read; the Marchioness of Salisbury; Watier; and of course, Robinson.

1

One never knows what sort of muddle the most idle of thoughts will land one in, now do they?

With nothing more than time on my hands one night, I pondered the seemingly innocent topic of the quality of the food at White's Club for gentlemen.

White's is the exclusive domain of four hundred fifty gentlemen who gather for intelligent conversation, a quiet corner in which to read a newspaper, a wager on a hand of cards, or a game of billiards. There are some wagers on less savoury topics involving the fair sex but, as a gentleman, I feel I should remain silent on those. Wringing your hands in frustration, are you? Well, I cannot be of service. As I said, I have my reputation as a gentleman to maintain.

At any rate, the one thing White's does not have is a decent chef. And that is a problem.

My harmless musings regarding the subject escalated to a crucial point when I swallowed yet another morsel of overcooked mutton, and my pained gaze met the identical one of Lord Headfort across the table.

"The animal must have been part of a flock of pugilistic sheep, this meat is so tough," I remarked, indicating my plate.

His lordship, a robust man in his fifties, chewed frantically, then swallowed using a great gulp of wine to wash the food down. "By Jove, Brummell, it's a sad day when a man can't come to his club and partake of a proper meal."

"Perhaps we ought to open another club and employ a chef who knows how to cater to a man's stomach," I reflected.

Sometimes a brilliant idea like that will pop into my head, you know.

Lord Headfort leaned forward eagerly. "I'll put money behind such an endeavour and help run the damn thing."

"And I shall be president," I replied selflessly.

No one can accuse me of being miserly. I am always generous when it comes to a good cause. Or a good plate of roast beef and Yorkshire pudding.

Over the following month—a delightful period of time when I sampled the efforts of various chefs—we hired a man named Watier and opened a club bearing his name at the corner of Piccadilly and Bolton streets.

Evidently Lord Headfort and I were not the only souls unhappy with the food at White's, for soon Watier's membership was at its limit.

Speaking of limits, past all previous limits was the amount of money a gentleman could gamble on macao, whist, or faro. How this happened, I cannot tell you. You do not think I had any part in raising the stakes, do you? Of course not.

All I know is that suddenly my club was renowned not only for its food, but it had the reputation for the most notoriously high level of play in London.

Unfortunately, where there is a great deal of money changing hands, there is often trouble.

On a warm evening in the first week of July, I sat at my usual table at Watier's—overlooking the door—partaking of a very fine Chambertin wine with Viscount Petersham. I enjoy a fine Chambertin, though most any good wine will do. My motto is: "When your spirits are low, get another bottle." Even when your spirits are not low, wine is good for a man's soul, I believe.

But I digress. I was speaking of my good friend Petersham. While we often debate the wisdom of his sporting side-whiskers, the viscount and I have been comrades since the late 1790s when we both served under the Prince of Wales in the Tenth Light Dragoons.

"Going to Vauxhall later tonight, aren't you?" he asked me.

"Good God, yes. Anything to relieve my boredom," I replied. I did not want to admit to myself that I had grown used to a new pastime: that of investigating murders. I cannot say that I am all that good at it, although I have stumbled my way through three previous cases. Without a killer to collar, life seems dull with only the cut of my coat, the graceful motion of raising my quizzing glass, and the exertion of having a witty remark on my tongue for my fellow members of Society. I occasionally require having something to stir the workings of my brain. You do know what I mean?

Petersham, who never leaves his house prior to six in the

evening, said, "The Pleasure Gardens at Vauxhall promise to be entertaining for once. All the world will be there, since it's a gala evening under the patronage of our Prince. There's to be a military review, a band, fireworks, and an exhibition of the Cascade."

"Intriguing," I replied absently, my attention caught elsewhere. "Devil take it, look who has just come in the door."

Petersham took the time to finish admiring his latest snuffbox—he has one for every day of the year—before raising heavy-lidded eyes to see what I was talking about. "You mean Sylvester Fairingdale?"

"Partly," I replied in a tight voice. "Though that fool will never overshadow me, no matter how much he wants to, not so long as he pairs glass-green breeches with a carrot-coloured coat."

"Everyone knows Fairingdale is a ninny. You aren't going to permit him to disturb your comfort, Brummell. Say, aren't those new breeches you've got on? Weston make them?"

"Yes," I answered shortly, for once not interested in disclosing the details of the creation of a new garment. I know this must shock you, but what can I say? That is how the matter stood. My gaze remained on Fairingdale and, more importantly, the young man he had in his company. Dressed in scarlet regimentals, the soldier was a good-looking youth with a square jaw and a wide smile.

Petersham managed to lean forward whilst expending the least amount of energy and pour himself another glass of wine. "How did Fairingdale obtain membership here at Watier's anyway?"

"My guard slipped, I expect. Anyway, I could not deny

him when he lives with Lord Wrayburn and the new Lady Wrayburn, remember?"

"Oh, that's right. No, the Wrayburns would take it as quite a snub."

"Besides, that coxcomb Fairingdale has left me alone for a while."

Petersham tsked. "Remember what you used to say to me when you'd protect me from the bullies who'd tease me about my asthma, 'Never let your guard down.' "

I watched the two men seat themselves at one of the tables and my heart sank. "I cannot believe it. Lieutenant Nevill is going to play again after all that happened last Saturday."

"Who's Nevill? The young fellow in the scarlet regimentals?"

I nodded, my gaze still on the table of gamblers. "After a spectacular loss at the tables just this past Saturday night, the youth declared he would place the business end of a pistol in his mouth and pull the trigger."

"No money, eh?"

"Not a shilling. I waived his debt. Then, I spent the better part of two hours convincing him that he need not end his life, that he should consider this a valuable lesson and not game beyond his means ever again."

"I say, that was good of you, Brummell."

I shrugged. "The lieutenant is a fine young man, not above twenty years of age. I could not let him commit such a heinous act as doing away with himself over a thousand pounds. What sort of fellow would I be? The club took the loss after Nevill said he would not play for high stakes again."

"Word is you rescued Tom Sheridan from a similar fate. Getting soft in your old age?"

I raised my right eyebrow. "I am only nine-and-twenty."
"And still unwed."

I motioned to a wigged footman for another bottle of Chambertin, leaving Petersham's comment hanging in the air. I do not have a wife and am not likely to obtain one any time soon. The lady I consider to be the Ideal, her Royal Highness, the Duchess of York, is married to another, devil take it. The other female in my life, Miss Lydia Lavender, is a high-spirited independent miss of the middle classes, who holds the Society where I am the Arbiter of Fashion in contempt. Besides, her father, a Bow Street investigator, would sooner have Napoleon for a son-in-law than yours truly, Beau Brummell.

Ignoring Petersham's words, I focused my attention on the lieutenant. Sure enough, he and Fairingdale had joined in a game. Blast! Had the young man not learned his lesson?

"Brummell, what are you going to do?"

"Do? Who am I, the Patron Saint of Fallen Gamblers?"

"Don't talk fustian. I can tell you want to go over there and yank Nevill from the table. Calm down. I don't see why you're worried. The other gamblers are unexceptional and won't let the play get too high. There's Lord Perry's cousin, Tallarico—"

"Whose only interest in life is females, I know."

"Exactly. And Theobald Jacombe. Come now, that man is beyond reproach. He won't lead young Nevill to ruin," Petersham opined, taking a pinch of snuff from his jewelled box.

I felt myself relax a bit. Petersham had the right of it. Theobald Jacombe is one of the most well-known, honourable men in London. He is the trusted friend of Earl Spencer and a long-time official in the Home Office. Mr. Jacombe oversees the magistrates of Bow Street and supports every effort to make London a safer place.

No, Lieutenant Nevill was in good hands. After the game, I would offer to buy him a drink and have another talk with him. All would be well.

I was wrong.

"You are a cheat, sir!" The accusation rang out across the green-baize tables, causing an instant silence to fall. A battery of shocked gazes turned toward the speaker.

I felt my heart plummet to my highly polished evening shoes. Lieutenant Nevill had been the speaker. He sat across from Mr. Jacombe and had accused that upstanding man. The youth's face was flushed red, though his bearing was proud and strong.

Mr. Jacombe's face paled with anger. "I beg your pardon," he said, deathly calm. "I could not have heard you correctly."

Victor Tallarico, an Italian now living in London and my only rival for the affections of the Duchess of York, uttered the words *"Dìo mío."*

The lieutenant glanced around the room nervously, but was not about to back down. "I saw you. You pulled a card from your sleeve. It's the oldest trick known to card players. Fellows in the barracks taught me that on the first day."

Everyone in the room sat riveted to the scene playing out in front of them.

"If you are well-versed in the ways of dishonest card-play, perhaps you are accusing me to cover your own perfidy," Mr. Jacombe said in a measuring tone.

Lieutenant Nevill shot to his feet.

By now I was at his side and placed a friendly hand on his shoulder. I applied pressure, gently forcing the soldier back into his chair while I addressed Mr. Jacombe. "Sir, how could our young lieutenant here be adept at cheating, when I see from his vouchers on the table and the number of gaming counters in front of you that he has lost a goodly amount?"

Mr. Jacombe is a paunchy man of middle years with sparse light brown hair and a fair complexion. He rubbed his chin in a considering manner. "Well, Brummell, that could be a way of disarming me. Nevill might have any number of schemes in mind. I've been around longer than you have, you know, and have heard the tales of men's trickery from the Bow Street magistrates. Nothing is above some men in their quest to advance themselves."

That put me in my place. Mr. Jacombe never has approved of me, thinking me a rackety sort trying to get above my place in life. He next eyed Petersham, who had come to stand beside me, with a faint air of contempt. Nothing obvious, mind you, but I am observant and noted it at once. Mr. Jacombe would not approve of the known close relationship Petersham has with his dearest companion, Lord Munro.

"Why not count the cards and settle the matter?" Lieutenant Nevill asked hotly.

"A good idea," Tallarico agreed.

Fairingdale remained safely silent, looking down his long nose at the company. The dolt.

Mr. Jacombe's deep-set blue eyes raked his accuser. "Because there is no need to lower myself to even consider responding to such a base accusation."

The lieutenant turned his gaze toward his saviour.

Er, that would be me.

"Mr. Brummell, sir. You can speak for me. When I lost all my money to you Saturday night, I obviously wasn't cheating. You knew that, else you wouldn't have dismissed my debt. Mr. Jacombe here is the one who is playing false." My hand was still on the youth's shoulder. I squeezed it a bit. "Often a man's eyes play tricks on him, Nevill. Why not give Mr. Jacombe the benefit of the doubt? Consider the game over and come have a drink with me."

I judged it best to end the matter before Nevill's accusation turned into a deadly confrontation. To say a man was a cheat could have only one inevitable consequence: a duel. Theobald Jacombe's reputation for honesty and fairness could be the only thing preventing him from thrashing the youth for questioning his honour. As it was, I could tell the government man was holding his temper in check with great effort.

Just then an oily voice sounded. "Had a run of bad luck lately, have you, Nevill?" Sylvester Fairingdale asked. "And Brummell let you off. How very kind of him. Did he make you give your word you would not play again?"

The lieutenant squared his shoulders, but my hand remained firm while I tried to contain him.

Fairingdale, with his forward-jutting chin and his unnaturally elongated neck, is one of those annoying people— really an adder—who breathes life through other people's misfortunes. I was not about to let him contribute his nastiness to an already dangerous situation.

I feel like an older brother to the naive lieutenant, protective and somewhat responsible for his continuing to draw breath in this life. "Financial matters of Watier's are nothing to do with you, Fairingdale."

Mr. Jacombe was not so easy to dispense with. "You discharged the soldier's debt to your club? Why?"

The word "compassion" sprang to my lips, but I bit it

back. "The lieutenant here is down on his luck. How was I to call in the debt? Have him shine my boots from now until eternity? My man, Robinson, would not have it. The valet considers his own abilities superiour to any other."

Lieutenant Nevill broke in. "Mr. Brummell is a gentleman," he declared passionately. "The epitome of a man of honour. He won more from me Saturday night than I could ever pay. The only path left to me was death. Brummell here talked me out of it. I owe him my life."

Mentally, I rolled my eyes at this impassioned speech. Was I ever this young and emotional? Yes, I had to admit, I was.

Mr. Jacombe's mouth puckered. He folded his arms across his barrel-like chest. "Yet here you are back at the tables again! The honourable thing is not to engage in a game of chance if you do not have the means with which to play. Give me one good reason why I should not challenge you to a duel for calling me a cheat."

At these lethal words, the occupants of the room froze in a stunned tableau.

2

While the room held its collective breath, my mind worked furiously. There must not be a duel. The lieutenant was sure to be the loser.

At the moment, his angular features were a study in deliberation whilst he contemplated how to answer Mr. Jacombe's question. Then he said, "I play because I must win funds to marry the woman I love."

"To marry?" Mr. Jacombe drawled in an incredulous voice. "What lady of good birth and breeding would marry a penniless soldier who loses at cards and then accuses a gentleman of cheating?"

"Her name is Molly, and she is the finest girl I know," the lieutenant spoke with pride.

Molly? I passed a hand over my eyes. She could not be the same Molly who repeatedly turned my household upside down last year by flirting with both of the twin men who carry my sedan-chair.

Mr. Jacombe tapped a beefy finger on the green baize. "Who is her father?"

Lieutenant Nevill swallowed hard. Underneath my fingers, I could feel his shoulders tense even more. Boldly, he spoke his mind. "Molly does not know who her real father is, nor her mother."

I drew a deep breath. When he was alive, my own father always criticised me, but at least I knew who he was. I felt a measure of sympathy for the young girl.

"I assume she is as penniless as you are," Mr. Jacombe spoke sharply.

"What has that to do with anything?" Lieutenant Nevill spoke without even trying to conceal his insolence. "She lives on her own at the Haven of Hope shelter and works hard to better herself."

Good God. The lieutenant's Molly was indeed the same girl I knew. If she were betrothed to the lieutenant, I could only assume she had given up her ways as a flirt, maturing as she grew older.

Mr. Jacombe appeared flustered for a brief moment. Then his expression turned thunderous. For an instant I thought he would strike the lieutenant, but he quickly regained his composure.

His voice was quiet, yet held an undertone of cold contempt. "The Haven of Hope? Everyone knows that is merely a cover for a brothel."

Like liquid fire rising from Hades, up through the soles of my black evening shoes, fury rose in me, making even my face feel the burn of its heat.

I am generally an easygoing sort, but my friend, Miss Lydia Lavender, whom I just mentioned to you as being one of the most important females in my life, runs the Haven of Hope shelter for women. Mr. Jacombe had just insulted a woman I hold in high regard in the most vile way.

Before I could control myself enough to say a word, however, the lieutenant shot to his feet once more. "That duel is in order after all! I shall not have you so abuse Molly, the woman I love."

He was right, I thought grimly, but perhaps I should be the one fighting the duel. Not many in Society know of my friendship with the middle-class Miss Lavender, but I could not let that be a factor now. The red-haired Miss Lavender's reputation was at stake as was Molly's.

"Mr. Jacombe, the Haven of Hope is not a brothel. I shall have to ask you to retract your statement," I said with a menacing calm.

"One of your favourite lightskirts there, Brummell?" Jacombe asked with a hint of scorn in his voice. "No, it won't do. This young soldier wants to face me down the length of a pistol—unless it is to be swords?—at Chalk Farm. Tomorrow morning then at dawn, Nevill?"

"Egad, dueling is illegal, Jacombe," Petersham tried.

But none of us paid attention.

"Will you act as my second, Mr. Brummell?" Lieutenant Nevill asked.

"Yes. I shall serve as your friend, though I would prefer to be the one firing the pistol," I replied. My gaze locked on Theobald Jacombe.

"I never had any quarrel with you, Brummell," Mr. Jacombe stated with a faint air of surprise.

"You do now," I stated.

The lieutenant rose from his chair, the wood scraping against the wood of the floor. The matter decided, he turned away and hurried out of the club without another word.

I looked at Mr. Jacombe, hardly bothering to conceal my disgust. How neatly he had turned an accusation against himself into a young man's defense of his love's honour.

"I'll be happy to stand as your second, Mr. Jacombe," Sylvester Fairingdale eagerly offered.

Mr. Jacombe nodded at him once. "Very well, Fairingdale. It's a shame about the soldier, but there was nothing else I could do."

I flashed him a look of disdain, words choking in my throat. There had been plenty he could have done to avoid this nightmare.

Undoubtedly, Mr. Jacombe was a better shot than the lieutenant, for the young man had told me he had not served in the military long, nor handled firearms beforehand. Then there was the fact that Mr. Jacombe was at least twice the lieutenant's age and therefore had twice the life's experience.

I felt the injustice of the situation as if it were the weight of a coach on my chest. A devilishly uncomfortable state of affairs, I assure you.

Mr. Jacombe gathered a group of his cronies and left the club, no doubt realizing I was about to throw him out.

Victor Tallarico ordered a bottle of port. "Have a drink, Brummell. You did what you could."

"He's right, Brummell," Petersham agreed. "Jacombe wants to fight."

Sylvester Fairingdale sat swinging his quizzing glass on its ribbon, obviously well-pleased with himself. For his consequence could only be raised by standing at the great Mr. Jacombe's side. Fairingdale and his plans were akin to a barking loon.

"Leave these premises at once, Fairingdale," I commanded him.

"In a moment," the fop said, examining the cards on the table.

All of a sudden he raised two cards.

Each was the king of diamonds.

I went to grab them from his fingers.

In a flash he pocketed them and, laughing, he dashed out the door.

I followed him outside, but the night was dark and the cad had disappeared. I punched my fist into my open palm, hearing my father's voice inside my head rebuking me for not preventing what might be a fatal confrontation for young Lieutenant Nevill.

Because of the meeting of the new Parliament, many families were in Town who ordinarily would not be. Add to that the fact that no less a personage than the Prince of Wales was hosting tonight's activities at Vauxhall Pleasure Gardens, and the result was a crowd in excess of four thousand people.

The twelve acres that make up Vauxhall Gardens appeal to all classes of Society. There is something for everyone to enjoy whether they be lovers seeking to steal a kiss in the Dark Walk, or just people out to hear the concert, view the fireworks, or enjoy the Cascade exhibition.

One can eat wafer-thin slices of ham and chicken in the supper boxes, watch the military band march, or promenade with friends down any of the numerous gravelled walks that are lit by hundreds of lamps, all for the price of admission: three shillings.

Perhaps the spirit of Vauxhall is best summed up in an

old ballad. I confess I cannot recall the author, but here it is:

> *Now the summer months come round,*
> *Fun and pleasure will abound,*
> *High and low and great and small,*
> *Run in droves to view Vauxhall.*
> *See the motley crew advance,*
> *Led by Folly in the dance,*
> *English, Irish, Spanish, Gaul*
> *Drive like mad to dear Vauxhall.*
>
> *Each profession, ev'ry trade*
> *Here enjoy refreshing shade,*
> *Empty is the cobbler's stall,*
> *He's gone with tinker to Vauxhall,*
> *Here they drink, and there they cram*
> *Chicken, pasty, beef, and ham,*
> *Women squeak and men drunk fall.*
> *Sweet enjoyment of Vauxhall.*

Upon my arrival in the Gardens that night, the Prince of Wales, or Prinny as he is called, had just begun marching a company of soldiers under his orders.

While Prinny has never seen a moment of battle, he persuades himself he is a great military man. Chiefly he designs his regiment's uniforms.

I saw Lieutenant Nevill was one of the chosen men tonight. Scanning the crowd watching the soldiers, I found Molly. Even from a distance, I could see her shining eyes as she gazed upon her beloved.

I heaved a sigh. How long would it be before that collective vulture known as Society knew about the impending duel? Of course the duel should be kept secret, which made it even more likely that the news would fly around Vauxhall faster than birds fly away from a predatory cat. No doubt Sylvester Fairingdale would do his part to make the news known.

Yes, there he was, whispering to beat the band, so to speak, to Lady Crecy, an older matron, kind enough, but with a propensity for gossip.

When Fairingdale left her side, I procured a glass of wine and walked up to the lady and bowed low. "Good evening, Lady Crecy. Are you enjoying the lovely night air?"

"Mr. Brummell! I have just had the most shocking news!" Lady Crecy proclaimed, her too-tight grey curls bouncing as she spoke. "It is being said that Mr. Jacombe, Mr. Theobald Jacombe, mind you, is to participate in a duel. Have you ever heard the like?"

"Never."

Lady Crecy's ample bosom heaved. "See there! That was precisely my reaction. Dear Mr. Jacombe would never involve himself in a duel."

"No?"

"Absolutely not. Why, he is the model of propriety. He is such a good man both in his public life and private. You know he has a wife who is practically an invalid. Yet he is the soul of patience with her. No wonder all of London respects and admires him."

"They do."

"I am certain this can be nothing more than a dreadful rumour. Mr. Jacombe himself will undoubtedly appear shortly and laugh away the very idea of his participating in such a nefarious activity. Oh! There is Mrs. Creevey. Mayhaps she knows something more about this. Will you excuse me, Mr. Brummell?"

"Of course." I watched her hurry away, and I drank the contents of my glass. All right, I admit I gulped it.

The military came to a pause in its review to a clapping of gloved hands. I took the opportunity to greet the Prince. Had word reached his ears about the duel? Did he know I was to stand as second to Lieutenant Nevill? If so, what would his reaction be?

"Brummell, well met."

"The troops are looking good tonight, your Royal Highness," I said, executing a low bow. "No doubt other troops are at this moment making Napoleon wish he never left Corsica."

The Prince of Wales, now above forty years of age, is my good friend. He has superb taste in the arts and has done much to enrich our country's supply of paintings, sculptures, and other works of art. He has created a palace in Brighton that will surely serve as a monument to him long after he has departed this life.

However, he can sometimes be overly dramatic and self-indulgent, the latter making itself known in the form of his ever-increasing girth. In fact, he was the very first to applaud the opening of Watier's and could frequently be found enjoying a repast there.

He smiled on me now. "Yes, the men are in fine form. Those silver-and-white dress uniforms for this evening were my creation. What think you of them?"

I bit my tongue, but not hard enough. "They are most eye-catching."

Prinny chuckled. "Thank you."

Now, you might know that my doctrine where a gentleman's clothing is concerned is that the greatest mortification a gentleman can endure is to call attention to himself by his dress. Simple elegance is preferred. Luckily, the slight had gone right over Prinny's royal head.

He glanced around, then looked me in the eye and said, "What is this I'm hearing about a duel between Jacombe and some army officer? None of the men in my regiment would participate in such low behaviour."

So Prinny did know. I could not betray Lieutenant Nevill, yet I could not lie to the Prince. "Just so, sir. I am certain if there is a duel, none of the men in *your* regiment would be involved."

There. Lieutenant Nevill was not in Prinny's regiment. He was only marching here at Vauxhall tonight to swell the numbers of soldiers. A simple play on words can sometimes solve a problem rather neatly.

The Prince's babyish face crinkled. "Doesn't seem right that Jacombe would fight a duel. He's a valuable man in the government and a decent shot as well." The royal gaze remained on me. "Are you going to tell me what happened, Brummell? I know you are this soldier's second."

I felt a tremor of uneasiness that I hope was not reflected on my face. "Sir, since this is a matter of honour, I am certain you must agree that it would be bad form for me to speak of it."

"Even to me?"

I considered this. "May I just say that the provocation was great on a young man suffering the throes of love."

I could tell this eased his mind. I knew it would. The Prince had once given himself a self-inflicted sword wound over a lady to convince her of his love. The ploy had worked, too.

"Love, eh? I can understand that. But you haven't told me why you are going to serve as this man's second, Brummell."

"Because I saved his life Saturday night," I explained. "He was going to end it all after gaming too high. I talked him out of it, and now I feel responsible for him."

There was no need to mention the added motive: that Mr. Jacombe had insulted Miss Lavender. My protective feeling toward the lieutenant was enough in and of itself.

Prinny nodded slowly. "Very well. But after the duel, you are to come directly to Carlton House and tell me what the devil happened."

"It shall be as you say, sir."

Just then, I saw John, Count Boruwlaski, a dwarf the Prince has befriended, walking in our direction. Standing only two feet and four inches, the Count's child-like size often causes Prinny to treat the man as a little boy. My patience with this sort of behaviour is, er, short.

"Excuse me," I began, but, his attention diverted, the Prince had already turned away to greet his friend. I walked in the direction of the soldiers, hoping for a word with Lieutenant Nevill. More precisely, I was hoping to convince him to abandon the idea of the duel and to send Mr. Jacombe a note of apology. I could fight the man myself. I did not have much hope for this plan, but I felt I must try.

I was halted in my tracks by the vision of Frederica, the Duchess of York, accompanied by her husband, Prinny's brother, the Duke of York. She saw me at the same time and offered me a small smile.

"Good evening, George," she said in her light, sweet voice. Tonight she wore an elegant gown of fine white India muslin, scalloped around the bottom and with long sleeves laced with gold twist. A bandeau made of pearls and white satin held her curly brown hair back from her face.

"Your Royal Highness, may I say how lovely you look tonight? More luminescent in that white gown than the moon."

"Thank you, George," she replied, one gloved hand entwined in the crook of her husband's arm. I felt a knot entwine around my heart at the sight of that hand.

Freddie, as I am privileged to call her in private, had been my closest female friend until recently. You might remember my telling you another time about that sordid situation regarding a letter from the Royal Duchess I foolishly kept and the murders it inspired. Yes? Well then you know that our relationship has been strained since that time.

The other impediment to any closeness between us stood next to her: her husband. The tall, cold man who is the Duke of York greeted me. "Brummell, what's this I hear about a duel between Jacombe and some nobody? Are you involved?"

Freddie's eyes rounded at her husband's words. She looked to me for an explanation.

My heart sank. How would Freddie feel about my being involved in a duel?

Unfortunately, I think I know.

Blast.

3

Damn Fairingdale. For I was sure he was the reason why every cursed person at Vauxhall knew about the duel. I felt my frustration increasing—and not just about the proposed pistols at dawn, I thought, as I gazed upon Freddie.

I especially did not want to speak of the duel to the Duke and Freddie. Being near her caused a longing for a return of our previous closeness. Any possibility of making amends would be put back even further if Freddie thought I was out fighting duels.

"Mr. Jacombe insulted a soldier's lady," I responded.

The Duke of York is the Commander-in-Chief of England's land forces. I hoped that by making it clear one of the duelists was a soldier, the Duke's curiosity might be satisfied.

"Who is he?"

"Lieutenant Nevill."

The Duke concentrated for a moment. "Never heard of him."

"His grandfather recently purchased a commission for him."

"Who is his grandfather?"

"Elsworth Nevill."

"What? Old Elsworth? I thought him six feet under, but no, stay a moment. He's a recluse, isn't he? Not been seen out of the house these past five years since his only son died."

"How terrible," Freddie said.

"From what I understand, that is true," I said. The lieutenant had said as much during that long talk Saturday night. "Lieutenant Nevill told me that his father drank himself to death over his mother's wild ways. She is somewhere on the Continent now. Young Nevill has not seen her since he was fourteen. I believe Elsworth Nevill holds her responsible for his son's death."

"I cannot understand how a mother could leave her child," Freddie said.

Her husband addressed her. "And you'll never know, since you've not given me an heir. All you have are dogs and plenty of those."

My body tensed. His tone of voice and his words infuriated me. How dare the Duke of York speak of his wife that way when he paraded his mistress, Mary Anne Clarke, in front of all of London? Poor Freddie. I wanted to strike her husband with the full force of my right fist.

Colour rushed into Freddie's face. I could see a hint of tears forming in her eyes.

That settled it. I looked at the Duke. "Your wife has one too many dogs."

His eyes met mine. He did not mistake my meaning. We stood that way, gazes locked, until the sound of the military band behind us forced our attention back to the troops on review.

The Duke turned without another word, Freddie still holding his arm, and walked away to stand next to the Prince of Wales, his brother.

I thought of going after him right then, of finally, after all these years, telling the Duke of York exactly what I think of the callous, dishonourable way he treats the most precious of women. Freddie. I thought of the pleasure I would derive out of connecting my fists with his flesh, of seeing him in pain for a change, rather than Freddie.

But then I remembered my precarious position in this Society of London, and more importantly who I am *not* to Freddie. It went down a bit hard, but there was the situation in a nutshell.

At least it appeared that, for the moment, she did not know of my involvement in the duel. If she did, she would surely have taken me to task.

"Mr. Brummell? Mr. Brummell, did you not hear me?"

I tore my gaze from Freddie to look at the woman beside me.

"Er, forgive me, Miss Lavender, my thoughts were elsewhere."

"I can see that," the Scotswoman said. Tonight she wore another of her sensible gowns, this one a dusky shade of grey. The colour complimented her dark red hair and emerald-like eyes.

But there was nothing fussy or extravagant about the gown. The directress of the Haven of Hope shelter for "destitute and downtrodden" females, as Miss Lavender is wont to say, is too busy to bother with feminine frills.

I made her a bow. "Are you enjoying the Pleasure Gardens

this evening?" I asked, hoping that Mr. Jacombe's words about the Haven of Hope had not reached Miss Lavender's ears.

"Yes, I am. I brought the girls from my shelter with me. I thought they deserved a treat. With the money Lord Perry gave me last year, I have been able to do more for them."

Lord Perry had given Miss Lavender a large sum of money to thank her for helping save his wife and baby during a difficult childbirth.

"How good you are, Miss Lavender. The girls are fortunate to have you and your establishment."

Miss Lavender's chin came up. "Someone must help them."

"I saw one of your charges here tonight. Molly."

Miss Lavender's lips curved upward. "I am proud of Molly. She has grown up. Remember how she used to flirt with your chairmen?"

"Yes."

"No doubt you've noticed she no longer behaves that way. In fact, she has found the most wonderful young man, and the two plan to marry."

"I recently became acquainted with Lieutenant Nevill."

"Oh, I didn't know that. I'm sure you must agree with my high opinion of him."

I nodded. Obviously word of the impending duel, and the reasons for it, had not reached Miss Lavender's ears. I would not tell her. The thought crossed my mind that she would appear at Chalk Farm at dawn and attempt to halt the proceedings.

Or no. Should the spirited Miss Lavender find out what Mr. Jacombe had said about her establishment, she would probably bring her own dueling pistol and face the man across the grass herself. Do you see why I like her? "Lieutenant Nevill is a bit rough around the edges, but a fine soldier," I said. "Since you say Molly has changed, and assuming she truly loves him, then the match is a good one." Miss Lavender smiled at me. Before we could continue our conversation, Lionel came dashing up to her side. Lionel is a boy of thirteen years, the only male Miss Lavender houses. She took him home after he had been arrested by her father for pickpocketing. Hunger had forced him to steal after he ran away from the master who had used him as a chimney-sweep in his younger years.

"Lionel, must you always race from place to place?" Miss Lavender scolded with affection.

His face split into a grin. "Iffen I'm to be a Bow Street Runner one day, I 'ave to keeps in practice. Evenin', Mr. Brummell, sir."

"Good evening, Lion," I said, using my nickname for him. He reminds me of a lion, with his wild mane of short, light brown hair that has streaks of blond at the top. One big cowlick in front serves only to accentuate his short nose. "Are you happy to have a night at Vauxhall?"

The boy grinned again. "I sure am. I'm told there's to be a great display of the Cascade tonight. I reckon that'll be mighty excitin'. Then the fireworks!"

I suddenly longed to be at Lion's side as he watched the Cascade exhibition and the fireworks display. Perhaps my jaded gaze would be able to appreciate the entertainments more if I viewed them through his eyes. "I am looking forward to the same activities. Why don't we watch them together?"

"Odsbodikins!" Lionel cried. He looked to Miss Lavender.

"Of course," I said, "I would be grateful for your company as well, Miss Lavender."

"I should like it above all things," she replied, eyes sparkling.

"Wait," Lionel said. "I almost forgots why I came to get you, Miss Lavender. Your father is over by the music pavilion with that starchy Mr. Read fella'. He wants you to come over."

Miss Lavender sighed. "Lionel, I've told you that Mr. Read is one of the important Bow Street magistrates. You must be polite to him if you wish for future employment with Bow Street."

"Yes, ma'am," Lionel muttered, his eyes downcast.

"Excuse us, please, Mr. Brummell."

"Certainly. Could we agree to meet back at this spot in a quarter of an hour? That should give us time to get a good place by the Cascade exhibition."

"Yes," she replied before walking away.

A sense of awareness caused me to turn my gaze toward the entrance of the Pleasure Gardens. A quieting of the crowd in that direction told me someone of significance had arrived. A moment later, Theobald Jacombe came into view. He was alone and bore an expression of confidence on his face.

All eyes were on him. He waved a hand as if in acknowledgment that everyone knew about the duel, and he was signalling that all was for a good purpose and would be well.

A spontaneous cheer went up as he made his way to the supper boxes. I could hardly believe my own ears. And there was Fairingdale, rushing to toady to Mr. Jacombe, to let everyone know that he was standing as Mr. Jacombe's second in the duel.

I procured a glass of wine and stood drinking the contents. Lieutenant Nevill must not fight this duel. I must convince him to withdraw. Then I could face Jacombe on my own. Intuition told me that a man of Jacombe's years who would fight a youth was a coward inside. The whole thing would be much too easy for him. What would be Jacombe's reaction if he were forced to fight me instead? I am more than a decent shot, if I say so myself.

With these thoughts firmly in mind, I sought out the lieutenant.

Yet another arrival caused a stir just as I was about to reach him. A very tall, thin man with hunched shoulders seemed to be the object of a great deal of whispering. I studied him, noticing first that he wore a long sable coat around his stringy body and a dark red velvet turban on his head, even though it was July. Past his seventieth year, the man's face was heavily lined and pinched-looking. His pale blue eyes scanned the ranks of soldiers before coming to rest on Lieutenant Nevill. From everything the lieutenant had told me, I judged this to be the young man's grandfather.

A breeze blew through the gardens at that moment, sending the ladies' gowns fluttering and the trees swaying. The old man wrapped the fur coat around his thin body even tighter. "Nicky," he called to the lieutenant.

Shamelessly, I decided to eavesdrop on the conversation. Lieutenant Nevill had told me his grandfather had purchased him a commission in the army but had refused to release funds for him to marry Molly. Recognizing that I knew only one side of the story, I wanted to hear what Mr.

Nevill had to say to his grandson. If I stayed in my place, pretending to observe a nearby juggler of oranges, I could listen. Then, if the opportunity arose, I might be able to use Mr. Nevill to help convince the lieutenant to withdraw from the duel. I can be clever upon occasion, you know.

Molly was with the lieutenant when his grandfather confronted him. The soldier started at the appearance of the older man. "Sir! I had no idea you would come to the Pleasure Gardens tonight."

"Neither did I." Mr. Nevill spoke in a raspy voice. "You are aware that I do not like leaving the comfort of my home to go about in the throngs of common people. But you forced me, Nicky. What the deuce is this I hear about you fighting a duel?"

The lieutenant's jaw dropped. "How did you—"

"Never mind how I found out," Mr. Nevill rasped, banging the tip of the cane he had been leaning on against the ground for emphasis. "How dare you drag our name through the mud this way?"

"Mr. Jacombe was cheating at cards," the lieutenant replied. He glanced at Molly standing at his side. I thought he must be loath to tell the rest of it within her hearing.

As it turned out, he did not have to.

"My eyes are not good anymore, as you know, Nicky, but my ears have not failed me. The reason for this duel is standing right next to you. You are a foolish boy. Theobald Jacombe will kill you and rightly so."

Molly coloured up. "Is he right, Nicky? Is the duel over me? You mustn't fight it, darling."

Mr. Nevill spoke, his voice rising an octave, before the lieutenant could answer. "You are the source of all this trou-

ble, missy. You will ruin my grandson the way his whore
of a mother ruined my son. He *is* fighting this duel because
of you! He is trying to win money to marry you, and now
feels compelled to defend your honour, what there is of it!"

Molly began to cry.

Lieutenant Nevill seemed torn between trying to comfort
her and addressing his grandfather. Handing Molly a handkerchief, he turned to face his relative. "Sir, if it weren't for
the fact that you refuse to release my inheritance to me, then
I wouldn't have been trying to gain money by whatever
means."

"Bah!" the older man cried. "If you were not so hot to get
a leg over this female, you would never marry her, hence
you would not have been gaming! From the word going
around, the place she lives in is nothing but a brothel, at
any rate. Why must you marry her? Bed her and be done
with her."

At that moment, several things happened at once.

Miss Lavender and Lionel returned to my side. Miss
Lavender heard Mr. Nevill's remarks about her shelter. I saw
her fists ball at her sides.

Molly burst into loud sobs at the idea that she might be
considered a lightskirt.

The lieutenant shouted at his grandfather. "I won't have
anything said against Molly, do I make myself clear? Mr.
Jacombe will meet me in the morning because he cheated
at cards and for his insult against my betrothed. It's bad
enough that you don't approve of the match between Molly
and me and refuse to help us, but if you join Mr. Jacombe
in bringing false accusations against her, I won't visit you
nor acknowledge you ever again."

The old man's face twisted, the lines creasing, his pale eyes hardening. "I leave you to your fate then, you stubborn boy. You are just like your father." With these words, he swung around and disappeared into the crowd.

4

Lieutenant Nevill led a sobbing Molly away down one of the walks.

I turned to Miss Lavender. Her expression was a blank, as if she were in shock. Her hands were still balled into fists at her sides. She stood staring at the spot where the confrontation between the lieutenant and his grandfather had taken place.

"Miss Lavender, are you quite well?" I asked.

"I'm fine," she replied, looking anything but all right.

"She done 'eard what that stupid old man said 'bout the 'Aven o' 'Ope," Lionel said unhappily. "Don't listen to 'im, Miss Lavender. 'E's so old, 'e prob'ly wouldn't know a whorin' place iffen 'e was to walk right in the door."

Miss Lavender turned in an odd, stiff manner to her young charge. "Stay here with Mr. Brummell. I'll return in a moment."

"Miss Lavender, where are you going?" I asked, anxious

because she was obviously deeply affected by the scene that had just taken place.

"I have some business to take care of," she said faintly. This tone of voice and demeanor were so out of character for the independent Miss Lavender, that I felt even more uncomfortable.

Before I could stop her, though, she had turned her steps toward the supper boxes.

I stood alone with Lionel, frustrated with myself. Events were spinning out of control. First I had not been able to speak to the lieutenant; now Miss Lavender had witnessed the ugly scene between the young man and his grandfather. Her reaction to it, though, was what was bothering me. I would have thought that upon hearing a slur on the name of her shelter, the young woman would have been quick to rise to its defense. Instead, she seemed withdrawn.

I confess I do not always know the ways of the female mind—far from it—but this incident with Miss Lavender was particularly baffling.

My thoughts were interrupted by the ringing of a bell.

"Ain't that the signal for the Cascade show, Mr. Brummell?" Lionel asked.

"Yes. We had best procure a place now. Come."

A mass of people were headed in the same direction, the northwest side of the gardens, to get a view of the Cascade. I looked for any sign of the lieutenant or Molly, but they had disappeared. Miss Lavender, too, was not in sight.

Twilight faded into darkness, causing the tiny lights that dot the garden to twinkle like the stars above us. The sounds of laughter grew louder, as the dim light incited the crowd to boisterous behaviour. A continuing breeze fluttered the green leaves of the trees all around us, sending the lanterns suspended from the branches swaying.

The Cascade exhibition boasts twenty-five-foot-tall arches, with curtains extending forty or fifty feet across the front. At precisely nine of the clock, the curtains would be drawn back to display a landscape scene illuminated by concealed lanterns. Though the exhibition lasted only a few minutes, it was popular.

With Lionel at my side, we reached a place very close to the front.

" 'Ere we are, Mr. Lavender, Mr. Read, sirs," Lionel said.

I swung around to find that I had inadvertently chosen a place near the Bow Street men. A mistake on my part.

Mr. Lavender is a stockily built man over fifty years of age. He has thick red bristly hair which, over the recent past, has been turning to grey. He wears not only bushy side-whiskers, but an enormous set of mustachios. Tonight, he was clad in the only type of clothing I had ever seen him wear: a black-and-white-speckled game coat with many pockets over well-worn corduroy breeches tucked into never-clean boots.

I wish he dressed better. He never obliges me.

He wishes I would leave his daughter alone. I never oblige him.

He eyed me with disfavor before grunting a greeting. "Mr. Brummell, I should have known you'd be here tonight, since the entertainments are under the patronage of the Prince. Where is your friend?"

Probably drinking and eating himself into a stupor somewhere, I thought uncharitably. "He should be here. The Cascade always appeals to him."

"Why aren't you with his Royal Highness?" Mr. Lavender asked.

"Because I knew you would appreciate my company more," I retorted.

Lionel sniggered.

Mr. Lavender pulled an ivory toothpick box from his pocket—one I had given him after he saved my life, an act I am sure he sometimes regrets—and spit on it. He then began to clean the box on the sleeve of his coat. This is a procedure he knows reduces me to a state of cringing horror. He then opened the box, plucked a thin wooden stick from it, and popped it in his mouth.

Apparently, having decided he had tortured me enough, Mr. Lavender introduced me to the man standing next to him. "This is Mr. James Read, our head magistrate at Bow Street."

"Good evening, Mr. Read," I said. He is a spare, short man, probably not three inches above five feet. His hair is completely white and, surprisingly for a man above sixty, not thinning. He wears the air of one in complete control of himself.

"A pleasure to make your acquaintance, Mr. Brummell," Mr. Read said without a trace of conviction behind the words.

Lionel rolled his eyes.

"Have you seen my daughter?" Mr. Lavender asked me in a tone that indicated he hoped my answer would be "no."

Knowing how much he would dislike a reply in the positive, I said, "Yes, we were together a short time ago and are to view the Cascade together."

Mr. Lavender growled. "Then where is she?"

I glanced around. "I am afraid I do not know. She said

she had some business to take care of. I assumed she meant
with one of her charges, since she brought the girls from
her shelter here tonight."

Saving me from any rebuke from her overly protective
father, the lady in question walked up to us at that very
moment. "Lydia, where have you been? I was worried," said Mr.
Lavender.

Miss Lavender still wore that distant, withdrawn look on
her face. I puzzled over it and could not understand what
had caused it. Mr. Nevill's damning words about her shelter
would be more likely to bring an outraged reaction in the
Scotswoman. Why was she behaving as she was?

"I've misplaced my shawl," she said.

"The Norwich one that belonged to Mrs. Lavender, God
rest her soul?" Mr. Lavender asked in a strong measure of
surprise.

"Yes. I've looked and can't find it. No doubt someone
picked it up."

"Where did you last have it?" I asked her.

"When father, Mr. Read, and Lionel and I were eating
supper in one of the boxes."

"I'll go look for it," Mr. Lavender said.

"Please do not trouble yourself," I told the Bow Street
investigator. He does not like my meddling in his affairs—
neither his work in solving criminal acts nor his daughter—
so naturally I try to thwart him at every turn. "The supper
boxes are just around the corner. I shall go."

Mr. Read ambled away, perhaps unwilling to watch Mr.
Lavender and me cross swords. Lionel was not so fainthearted
and stood grinning.

"No, I will go," the bluff Mr. Lavender insisted.

I assumed a nonchalant air. "Well, I hold myself honoured that you would leave Lionel and me here to protect your daughter in this crowd. There is Sylvester Fairingdale only a few steps away, I see. You know he can be relied upon for assistance should any of the rowdy young bucks take a fancy to your daughter's stunning red hair and try to steal a kiss."

A chuckle escaped from Lionel.

Mr. Lavender stood silently glaring at me. I imagined him grinding his teeth against the toothpick as that object jerked up and down in his mouth.

Miss Lavender remained aloof from the conversation. So unlike her.

"Oh, do as you want, Mr. Brummell," Mr. Lavender finally said, burring his *r,* a sure sign of irritation.

I nimbly made my way over to the nearly deserted supper boxes. After a careful search, I could find no shawl. Expecting any moment to hear cheers from the crowd at the Cascade exhibition, I was surprised as the minutes ticked by and no such sound occurred.

When I returned to the Lavenders and Lionel some fifteen minutes later, it was to see the Prince standing by the side of the exhibition, just about to announce its opening. I had not missed anything. Except Mr. Lavender's scorn when I returned empty-handed.

By some unheard signal, the crowd suddenly went silent. The Prince of Wales's voice rang out over the night. "Ladies and gentlemen, as we stand here in the greatest city in Europe, nay, in all the world, in the middle of summer, I offer you a glimpse of the Alpine mountains in all the glory of winter. Let the Cascade begin!"

A cheer went up.

Slowly, the heavy curtains were pulled aside revealing, to everyone's pleasure, a large backdrop painted in startling, vivid colours. The scene was of a snowy mountain, the green trees laden heavily with bright white snow. A tiny village had been carefully painted in the foreground.

However, it was the exquisite waterfall that held one in its thrall. Made of tin, it had been bent, shaped, and hammered to give the illusion of water flowing. This illusion was made more realistic by the softly glowing lights and chunks of tin painted white and embedded with chips of glistening glass which lined the sides of the waterfall.

From somewhere behind the display, a mechanism began to turn the roll of tin so that water appeared to be flowing down the mountainside. Shaved flakes of what I guessed were soap rolled down along with the "water" to resemble snow. Murmurs of approval went through the delighted crowd as the illusion charmed everyone.

But then I thought our pleasure might be spoiled as an odd bumping sound came from behind the waterfall. The clamour sounded like the mechanism was grinding and tugging on something. Others heard it, too, as the crowd's din of approval ceased.

Our attention flew to the top of the waterfall, where a grey bulky object was poised at the summit, ready to come down.

And down it came, revealing itself to all and sundry as the body of a man. Down the glimmering waterfall the body fell in a twisted, tumbling heap, sprinkling spots of red on the glossy tin in its path. Down to the pool of snow at the bottom where brilliant red bled into the icy white.

Over the stunned silence of the crowd, a single scream

sounded from somewhere behind the exhibition.

Mr. Lavender rushed forward and turned the dead man over.

Theobald Jacombe had been shot through the heart.

❧ 5 ❧

A chorus of echoing screams erupted from the crowd.
Ladies fainted.

A gabble of panicked voices rose around me.

James Read pushed past people who had surged forward
for a closer look at the macabre scene. A few quick words
passed between him and Mr. Lavender.

The Scotsman then hastened toward the rear of the exhibition, no doubt to find the source of that other scream.
Mr. Read kept the curious from getting too close to the
body. Constables patrolling the gardens rushed to aid him.

I looked first to Miss Lavender. Her mouth was open, her
eyes fixed on the dead man. I placed my gloved fingertips
through the crook of her arm. "Miss Lavender, let us move
away."

"Is he dead?" she asked faintly.

"Yes."

"Are you sure?"

"Quite."

She tilted her head, her emerald gaze riveted on Mr. Jacombe's body.

I gently tried to pull her in my direction, but she remained rigid.

On her other side, I could see Lionel swallow hard. " 'E's dead, Miss Lavender. 'E won't be walkin' the streets again, I can tell you, 'cause I seen a lot durin' my life."

"All thirteen years of it," I said, placing some emphasis on the words. I hoped the reminder would serve to break the spell the scene in front of us had over Miss Lavender.

The ploy worked. She turned slowly to him. "Lionel, find the girls. We must all leave together. That would be best," she told him haltingly, as if it were an effort to form coherent thought. "Have everyone gather at the entrance to the gardens. Run now."

"Not yet," the boy protested. "I 'ave to keep you safe. As to that man, good riddance to bad rubbish is what I says."

"It's Theobald Jacombe who's been killed!" Sylvester Fairingdale shouted the obvious to those who could not see. Another instance of him only wanting to start trouble.

Immediately, an increase in the volume of voices resulted.

"Fairingdale, cannot you see we shall have a panic on our hands with this crowd at any moment? Do not make matters worse," I said.

More constables appeared on the scene.

But there was no stopping Fairingdale.

Raising his voice, he cried, "You won't have to serve as second in that duel now, will you, Brummell?"

"Nor will you," I stated in a tone one reserved for a child of five years.

"At least I was Mr. Jacombe's friend," the fop cried, making sure his voice carried. People around us had stopped their own conversations to listen. "I wonder who could have done this to such a good man?"

Nodding heads and murmurs of agreement went through those nearby.

"It's outrageous!" a voice called.

"Jacombe was one of England's finest men," another declared.

"Who killed him?" someone asked.

"Whoever murdered him will be hanged!" declared a stout man.

Fairingdale needed no more to fuel his speech. "In our supper box just a short time ago, a boy came and delivered a note to Mr. Jacombe. Mr. Jacombe left our table after reading the note and never returned. Undoubtedly it was a note from the killer. Why, the boy in question might have been that one right there!" he ended, extending his arm and pointing a finger at Lionel.

" 'Tweren't me!" Lionel exclaimed.

"You'd hardly admit to it," Fairingdale retorted.

" 'Tweren't me!" Lionel shouted at him again. He took up a fighting stance in front of Fairingdale.

"You are talking nonsense, Fairingdale," I said. "You have consumed so much wine you would not know one boy from another. Cease your accusations."

"I am only pointing out the obvious," Fairingdale said stubbornly.

"There is nothing obvious here other than that a man is dead," I countered.

Out of the corner of my eye, I noted Mr. Read listening to our conversation. Devil take Fairingdale.

"Go find the girls, Lionel," Miss Lavender intervened. "No one believes you to have delivered any note."

"Yes, ma'am!" Lionel cried. Shooting Fairingdale a belligerent look, the boy hurried away.

Fairingdale turned a curious eye toward me. "Whoever killed Jacombe had time enough to come around to the front of the Cascade. Perhaps you've already served as that soldier's friend, Brummell."

I took three steps until I was directly in front of him. "Unless you want me to introduce your nose to my right fist, you had best cease prattling dangerous nonsense. I have been standing right here—"

"Nay. You disappeared from the company for a good quarter of an hour, right before Jacombe's body came over that waterfall. You had plenty of time to kill him, and so I shall tell Bow Street."

Anger and frustration welled up in me. "You are the most unprincipled man I have ever had the misfortune to know. You will stop at nothing in order to discredit me, will you, Fairingdale?"

The fop looked down his nose at me. "I shall lead Society one day."

"No, you will not. Even if I died tomorrow, you could never take my place. You have no character, no sense of style, no honour."

"We'll see about that." Fairingdale's face turned into a glowering mask of rage. He stepped over to Mr. Read and began speaking with the Bow Street magistrate.

Even though I knew Fairingdale's word would not be taken seriously, it rankled that Mr. Lavender would have to hear my name spoken in such a way.

At my side, Miss Lavender spoke. "What is that awful man trying to do, Mr. Brummell? Is he saying you killed

Jacombe? What is happening? I confess my head is spinning."

I put a protective arm about her shoulders. "Do not be anxious, Miss Lavender. Fairingdale shall not get the better of me."

"You couldn't have killed him. You didn't know what he—"

Whatever Miss Lavender was going to say would have to wait. For at that moment, her father appeared from behind the Cascade. An army of constables was with him.

Mr. Lavender, a grim expression on his face, held Lieutenant Nevill by the arm. A sobbing Molly trailed behind them.

The young soldier tried to give the appearance of confidence, but there was fear in the back of his pale blue eyes.

" 'Tis Nevill!" Fairingdale bellowed. "The soldier who was supposed to fight a duel with Mr. Jacombe in the morning. He decided the outcome of the duel tonight, it seems. He murdered Mr. Jacombe!"

A roar went up in the crowd. Behind me I could feel people pressing forward. I tightened my protective grip around Miss Lavender's shoulders. The ring of constables around the lieutenant made sure no one got close. As they passed, shouts rang out.

"Coward!"

"Murderer!"

"Hang him!"

6

Good God, what had happened? The lieutenant could not have killed Mr. Jacombe. I refused to even consider it. The duel was set. He would never commit a cold-blooded murder in order to avoid it.

Additional constables joined the ring around Mr. Lavender and his prisoner, more to protect them from the angry crowd than to keep the young soldier from bolting.

After a few words with Mr. Lavender, one of the constables broke off to speak to Mr. Read. That man nodded his agreement to the words spoken, and the constable rushed back to Mr. Lavender.

All this happened in the space of a minute. Then the lieutenant was led away. Molly screamed his name between sobs.

I raised my voice. "Molly!"

The girl saw me standing with Miss Lavender and hurried to our side. I had to pull my arm from around Miss Lavender when Molly threw herself into Miss Lavender's arms, sobbing her heart out.

The crowd began to disperse, some following Mr. Lavender and his prisoner, some remaining in order to get a glimpse of the body. One of Mr. Read's men found a cloth and laid it over Mr. Jacombe.

I judged it best to lead the ladies toward the exit where Lionel should be waiting with the other girls from the shelter. I desperately wanted to question Molly, but the girl was obviously hysterical. I would have to give her a few minutes.

"Let us move away from this gruesome scene," I said, pulling a handkerchief from my pocket and handing it to Molly.

She wiped her face and clung to Miss Lavender's arm. I placed a hand at Miss Lavender's other elbow and carefully guided our steps out of the Cascade area.

When we passed by the now empty supper boxes, a glimpse of a paisley design caught my eye. There was Miss Lavender's shawl. I recalled a couple had been seated in that particular box before, so I could not have seen it.

I released her arm for a moment and picked up the shawl. "Here, a little worse for its ordeal, but I think you can clean it."

"Thank you." Miss Lavender accepted the shawl gratefully. Despite its soiled condition, she put it about her shoulders, hugging it tight.

"Shall we sit here for a moment, ladies? Lionel is probably still gathering the other girls," I said.

The idea was quickly agreed upon. I saw them seated in one of the boxes, then I noticed a footman closing up a refreshment booth.

Telling the ladies to remain where they were, I procured

two glasses of ratafia for them and a glass of wine for myself and sat across the small round table from them. Once Molly had taken a few restorative sips, I began my questioning.

"Now, Molly, can you tell us what happened?"

The girl's eyes welled with tears, a gulping sob escaping her lips. Her shiny dark hair was coming out of its pins, her pretty, wholesome looks marred by swollen eyes and tear-stained cheeks.

She used the handkerchief I had given her, then spoke. "After that horrid scene with his grandfather, Nicky and I just wanted to be alone. We were going to get something to eat, but the supper boxes were crowded. So Nicky led me to the grassy area behind the Cascade exhibition where we could be completely private."

"No one else was back there?" I asked.

She shook her dark curls. "No one really. The man who turns the crank that makes the waterfall turn was there. But it was very dark. We stayed in the shadows. Anyway, he was drunk and singing to himself. I think he was oblivious to everything going on about him. By the time your father came around the exhibition, Miss Lavender, the operator was unconscious."

Miss Lavender nodded. She was being very quiet. The demeanour she had adopted from the time she first heard the lieutenant's grandfather's condemnation of her shelter was still in place.

I looked at Molly. "So the two of you were back a bit from the actual operation of the Cascade."

"Yes. Nicky and I were talking . . . and, well, kissing, you know. We are betrothed."

"Of course."

Molly took another sip of her drink. "I was trying to talk

Nicky out of that duel. I was so afraid for him!"

"Of course you were. I applaud your efforts. In fact, I was trying to find him, so I could talk to him along the same line of thinking."

"You're a good friend, Mr. Brummell."

"What happened next?"

Molly looked to one side as if seeing everything in her mind's eye. "Nicky said he had to fight the duel. His honour was at stake, as well as mine. Then we were kissing again when we heard the shot. At first we didn't know what it was, perhaps fireworks. It was just a loud noise nearby that startled us. We drew apart and saw a figure run past us in the shadows."

"A figure?" I said, leaning forward in my chair. "A man or a woman?"

Molly shook her head. "As I told Miss Lavender's father, it all happened so fast, and it was so dark back there. Neither Nicky nor I could tell whether it was a man or a woman. There was just the blur of a person running. That's all."

I nodded, concealing my disappointment. "That is understandable. Go on."

"Well, Nicky and I moved toward the Cascade. The operator was slumped over in his chair, but then . . . but then we saw—"

She broke off, tears choking her. Miss Lavender made soothing noises while placing an arm about the girl's shoulders and hugging her.

When Molly had control of herself again, she said, "It was awful. We looked up and saw Mr. Jacombe—only we didn't know it was him then—we saw that he was caught in the mechanism that makes the big waterfall move down the mountain. His body was being lifted and sent over the side. I screamed when I saw it."

I remembered hearing that scream right after the thudding sound. "What did you do then?"

"I just stood there. Nicky put his arms around me, then he told me we had to get out of there, but he stepped on something. It was the gun, Mr. Brummell. The killer had left the gun behind. I remember thinking how small it was for something so deadly."

"Indeed."

"Nicky picked the gun up from the grass. He said it was warm. We figured out that someone had shot the man. I was so scared, but Nicky said we would turn the gun over to Bow Street and tell them what happened. But then there was all the screaming from out front."

"Mr. Jacombe's body had come over the waterfall," I told her.

Miss Lavender trembled.

Molly continued. "Then all I know is that there was a man, I don't know who he was. He was finely dressed, so I expect he was of the Nobility. He saw us standing there. Then Mr. Lavender came and saw Nicky holding the gun."

I closed my eyes. How much more damning could the situation be for the lieutenant?

I opened my eyes and looked at Molly. "I assume you and Lieutenant Nevill told Mr. Lavender everything you just told me?"

"Yes. I am to report to Bow Street in the morning to tell everything I know again. I don't know why."

"That is normal procedure, Molly," Miss Lavender said.

"What about the other man? The one you said was of the Nobility?" I asked.

Molly shook her head. "I don't know who he was. Mr. Lavender spoke to him and took notes. Then Mr. Lavender said he was taking Nicky into custody on suspicion of murdering Mr. Theobald Jacombe."

Molly burst into fresh tears. "That's the first we even knew who the killed man was! I swear it!"

"We believe you, don't we, Mr. Brummell?" Miss Lavender said.

"Yes," I agreed.

Molly spoke through her tears. "It doesn't matter though, because your father doesn't believe us, Miss Lavender. I'm so afraid! They'll hang Nicky!"

7

When I woke early—around ten—the next day, my first thought was of Lieutenant Nevill. The problem with this murder investigation, I decided, was that there were no other obvious suspects. The lieutenant had been found literally with the gun in his hand, so Bow Street would not even be looking for anyone else.

I had not been well-acquainted with Theobald Jacombe. So my task would have to be to find out more about him. Specifically, who would want to kill a man with a spotless reputation.

First, though, I wanted to see if Bow Street was still holding the lieutenant. I hoped he had not been sent to prison, but it was a frail hope.

The door to my bedchamber opened. As all good menservants should, my valet, Robinson, had somehow perceived that my eyes were open. He entered holding a tray containing a pot of tea and some rolls. Later, after I had bathed and completed The Dressing Hour, I would have a proper breakfast.

"Good morning, sir," Robinson intoned. He was dressed as meticulously as yours truly in one of my old dark blue coats cut down to fit him. His build is slightly smaller than my tall frame. His blond hair was carefully combed into the Brutus style and his lips were pursed. The cause of this sign of disapproval laid in the centre of my bed: Chakkri.

Chakkri is the only Siamese cat in England. He is leaner than most cats I have ever seen and extraordinarily graceful. His colouring is a fawn tone, except for his face, paws, ears, and tail. These are a rich velvet brown. His eyes are his most remarkable feature, though. They are an incredible shade of rich blue.

This unusual animal was given to me by a Siamese emissary who visited England almost two years ago. Mr. Kiang had left the cat with me, along with a cryptic note saying Chakkri reminded him of me. I still do not know what he meant by it. Perhaps if you are so inclined, you can puzzle it out.

Chakkri had been engaged in his own morning ritual of bathing. His pink tongue efficiently washed his fawn-coloured body. He licked his right paw well, then used it to clean his whisker pad.

I approved of his fastidiousness, but Robinson, on the other hand, could find no redeeming qualities in the feline. The valet spends countless hours removing cat hairs from every surface in my well-appointed chamber. Furthermore, he has a special cloth he uses to eradicate any cat hairs that dare attach themselves to my clothing. Robinson has his reputation as a valet to maintain, you know. Needless to say, he wishes the cat, and all his troublesome cat hairs, to be placed in a crate and shipped back to Siam.

I sat up in bed and accepted a cup of steaming hot tea. "A bad business last night, Robinson. Theobald Jacombe was murdered."

Chakkri let out a low "reow," stood up, turned around twice, then curled into a ball with one paw firmly across his eyes. This was unusual behaviour. Normally Chakkri watches his surroundings with acute interest.

Robinson averted his gaze from the cat and looked instead at me. "Sir, I know. I saw the whole thing happen."

I replaced my teacup on the tray with a clatter. "What did you say?"

"When you gave me the evening off last night, I attended Vauxhall, just as you had said you planned to do. I went with Rumbelow, the underbutler—"

"Yes, yes, I know who your friends are. Get to the point, man."

"We were standing in front of the Cascade, waiting for the exhibition to begin. Rumbelow began telling me how fig-leaves boiled in water were the best for removing stains from silk handkerchiefs. When I pulled my handkerchief out to show him how much better spirits of turpentine are to achieve cleanliness, the silk slipped from my fingers. Then the wind picked up the material and I, er, had to chase the handkerchief. Rumbelow thought my predicament humourous."

"All right, so you ended up behind the Cascade when the murder took place. Who did it?"

Robinson shook his head. "I do not know. I heard a popping noise, but thought it was part of the exhibition. The only thing I saw back there was a soldier and his ladyfriend. He was holding a gun."

"Good God. Never say that is what you told Mr. Lavender?"

Robinson looked down his nose at me. "Was I to lie?"

I groaned out loud. Then it occurred to me that Robinson had been the "member of the Nobility" Molly had referred to as having seen her and Lieutenant Nevill. Of course she would think Robinson a peer, dressed as he was in my fine castoffs and with his haughty demeanor. This would be funny if the situation were not so serious.

"No, you were not to lie. But, Robinson, think hard. Was there no one else?"

"No, sir. Except the drunken man employed to operate the Cascade. Why?"

"Because the soldier is a friend of mine, Lieutenant Nevill. He was to participate in a duel this morning with the deceased. I was to act as his second."

"A duel?" Robinson's eyes shone. He loves drama and a good gossip. In fact, I am surprised he had not already heard of the duel.

"Obviously there is no need for it now. Furthermore, the young lady he was with is a friend of Miss Lavender's and, in fact, lives with her at the Haven of Hope."

"Dear me," Robinson said.

I raised my right eyebrow severely. "Do not take that tone in regards to Miss Lavender. She is a fine female, one worthy of your respect. And she is lovely, in addition to having a fine character. You should not judge her ill because she flaunts some of Society's conventions. Recollect that she is not a member of the *Beau Monde,* but of the middle classes."

"*I* remember, sir. Do you?"

I frowned. "Just what is that remark supposed to mean?"

"You do seem to enjoy Miss Lavender's company. I do not think it will serve, sir."

"You do not think what will serve?" I demanded.

"Falling in love with Miss Lavender."

My heart performed an odd thump. "Of all the impertinence! I am not in love with Miss Lavender. Now go downstairs and have Ned and Ted help you bring the water for my bath. I have no wish to speak to you further. And find out from your league of butlers, maids, and footmen friends where Lieutenant Nevill is being held. I am certain London is talking of nothing else this morning."

"Yes, sir," Robinson said. Then, with a back as stiff as a tree trunk, he exited the room, closing the door none too quietly.

You may be wondering why I put up with such nonsense. Well, all I can tell you is that Robinson has been with me for some years now. He has a high moral character I admire, he is intelligent and loyal, has a remarkable sense of style, and excels in his duties. Naturally, I would not want him to know I feel this way, so pray do not tell him. He is haughty enough as it is.

While Chakkri slept peacefully—he knew breakfast would be forthcoming—I contemplated the valet's involvement in the events of last night.

So Robinson had given a statement to Mr. Lavender. Of all the coincidences in the world, why did my very own valet have to stumble upon the scene of the crime? How would his statement affect the investigation? Not well. For now Bow Street had Mr. Lavender, one of their top men, and Robinson as witnesses. Both had seen Lieutenant Nevill with the murder weapon in his hand.

But they had not seen him shoot the gun.

Perhaps that fact alone would give me enough time to figure out who had fired the pistol. Surely Bow Street could not rush to indict the lieutenant without more solid proof of his guilt.

Later that morning, after I was faultlessly attired in a slate-blue coat, buff breeches, white waistcoat, and cravat, I breakfasted in the dining room. Chakkri dined as well, enjoying his favourite scrambled eggs in cheese sauce that my French chef, André, prepares for the spoiled feline.

Robinson entered the room.

I looked at him over the newspaper. "Yes, what have you found out?"

"Sir, Lieutenant Nevill is being held at King's Bench Prison. Word is, his commanding officer released him into the custody of Bow Street."

"I expect it was too much to hope for anything else. Still, it makes things even darker for the lieutenant that his military superior apparently did nothing to keep him from gaol. At least they did not take him to Newgate." I shuddered at the thought of that terrible place. I must go at once to talk to the young man.

We were interrupted at that moment by a ferocious pounding at the front door. Robinson steeled himself and exited the room.

A moment later, I could hear a crusty female voice shout, "I'll see my boys, and no starched-up prig'll stop me!"

I put down my newspaper and left the dining room. From the top of the stairs, I saw an astonishing sight: a tiny grey-haired woman in a homespun brown dress held a brown and white piglet in her arms. A portmanteau—if one could call the dusty, torn case that—stood at her feet. The hem of her gown ended several inches above her ankles, revealing men's work boots.

Robinson's face was as white as my cravat.

"What is going on here?" I asked, descending the stairs. "Who is this, Robinson?"

The valet turned to me with a stricken expression on his face. The pig squealed, the sound reverberating off the walls and black-and-white-tiled floor. "Ned and Ted's mother."

I studied the country woman. So this was "Mum," whom the two country boys worshiped. They sent home their chairmen's pay to her every quarter and often extolled the virtues of the woman who ran their family pig farm alone. Now here she was in London to see her boys.

"You must be Mr. Brummell," she said in that crusty voice. Her gaze ran the length of me. She let out a loud snort. "I can't see 'ow the likes of you 'as been takin' good care of my boys."

The pig squealed in agreement.

I managed to find my voice. "I assure you the twins are thriving."

"That's not what I 'ear. They were fightin' over some girl a while back. I 'ear tell all is right between 'em again, but I 'ad to leave my farm to come up and check on 'em. Boys will be boys."

"Er, indeed," I said, noting that Robinson swayed. "I beg your pardon, but I do not think I know your name, Mrs. . . ."

"I'm Edwina. But call me Ed. Everyone does."

"Mrs. Ed," Robinson uttered.

The piglet squealed again.

The sound brought Ned and Ted from the kitchen. There followed a scene of joyful reunion between a mother and her children. Ned and Ted are identical twins, both tall, blond, and with muscular physiques. Robinson says that between them they do not have the intelligence of a turnip.

Ted said, "You don't mind if Mum stays with us awhile, do you, Mr. Brummell, sir?"

Robinson cut me a pleading look, his blue eyes starting from his head.

"I won't be no trouble to yer," Mrs. Ed assured me. "Winifred here and I'll jest sleep out back with the horses."

Winifred? The piglet had a name?

"We do not keep horses," I told her.

She drew back her head and looked at me as if I were a cave dweller. "Don't keep horses?"

"No," Robinson said. "We do not have a stable, so you see, it would be quite out of the question—"

Ned, the garrulous twin, interrupted him. "Oh, that won't matter. Mum can stay in our room in the attic," he said with a big grin. "We'll 'ave the best time. It'll be like when we were younger, won't it, Mum? You can cook for us, too. We've 'ad to eat all that Frenchie's cookin'. Not that I don't like Mr. André, but 'e 'as to pour sauce over everythin'. Can't make a plain plate of eggs nor a good piece of boiled beef. I don't know why. Mayhaps sauce is in his blood." Ned snickered at his own joke.

Mrs. Ed eyed her boys. "Ye both do look like yer in need of feedin' up. My arthur-itis 'asn't been givin' me trouble lately. Reckon I could 'elp out while I'm 'ere. I'll teach the Frenchie about good English cookin'," she said with a smile that revealed all four of her teeth.

Robinson clutched the door frame in one white-fisted hand.

The twins looked at me expectantly.

"Certainly, I have no objection to your paying your sons

a visit. I hope you will be comfortable upstairs with them. Er, do you wish my man to make provisions in the back garden for, er, Winifred there?"

Robinson put a hand to his heart.

Mrs. Ed shook her head. "No, sir. She'll do fine with me in the attics. She was the runt of the litter. I've taken a fancy to 'er. She can sleep in my bed."

Robinson reeled from this blow.

I judged it best to make my escape now before another moment passed. "Well, I shall leave you to settle in. Robinson, make sure Mrs. Ed has everything she requires. I must go to King's Bench Prison."

Mrs. Ed swung around to face me, a suspicious look on her withered features. "King's Bench Prison? Yer not in any trouble, are ye?"

I took one look at Robinson's seething countenance. I thought of André being instructed in the fine arts of cookery by Mrs. Ed. I thought of my fashionable Town house housing a piglet.

Most importantly, I thought of the young soldier imprisoned for a heinous crime I knew he had not committed. I thought of how all of London was crying for conviction of Mr. Jacombe's murderer, and I feared for Lieutenant Nevill's life.

"No, I am not in any trouble. None at all."

❧ 8 ❧

During the Gordon Riots, King's Bench Prison had
been burnt to the ground, then quickly rebuilt. Arriving in
St. George's Fields, I noted the large new, but cheerless
building with its open courtyard surrounded by a high wall.

When I inquired about Lieutenant Nevill, the blustery
guard informed me that many had asked to see him, but he
had orders to keep the curious away. Only after several coins
changed hands was I admitted.

I walked down the damp, evil-smelling hall, listening to
the cries and ravings of the prisoners. My heart sank when
the guard showed me where the young soldier had been
placed. A square cell, no bigger than my dining room, held
two dozen souls in squalor.

Every sort of rough customer was represented. A beefy
man held a skinny ruffian against one wall, methodically
pummeling the latter's stomach with blows. Insects
marched across the floor toward a tray of soured food.

Lieutenant Nevill sat in a far corner, dressed in his shirtsleeves, his back to the wall, his knees drawn up against his body. He held his head in his hands.

"Lieutenant Nevill!" I called.

All eyes turned to me. A rush of bodies came toward the iron bars. Hands extended out to me, but I kept myself out of reach.

"A shilling or two, sir, please?" an older man begged.

"Would ye need a valet? I didn't kill me last master, I swear."

"Gin, I just need a swallow or two."

The lieutenant pushed his way to the front. His shirt was torn down one sleeve, his left cheek was bruised, and the knuckles of his right hand were caked with blood. "Mr. Brummell, sir! How glad I am to see you."

"Ooooh, the famous dandy," a voice cried.

Several men executed mock bows. I gripped my dog's head walking stick, the one Freddie had given me that contains a deadly swordstick. "I shall return in a moment, Lieutenant Nevill."

So saying, I went to find the guard. He sat on a high stool at the end of the grey hallway, drinking from a tin cup. He ignored my approach.

"I want a private cell for my friend, Lieutenant Nevill," I stated.

That got his attention. "It'll cost yer."

There followed a round of negotiations, the intensity of which could have rivaled any talks of peace between England and France. At last, a price was agreed upon, which included decent meals for the young soldier.

We walked back down to the grimy cell. With much pushing, swearing, and shoving, the guard extracted the lieutenant from his fellow inmates. He led us through a set of equally depressing halls until we reached a quiet one. Wooden doors with iron locks lined the area. Selecting a key from a large ring, the guard opened one of the doors and let us in.

While not exactly the sort of accommodations found in St. James's Palace, the room was relatively clean. A small bed was even tucked against a corner.

"Return in half an hour," I told the guard.

He left us alone, locking the door behind him.

"Mr. Brummell, your generosity is very sincerely appreciated. Thank you," the young soldier said.

"Let us hope we can remove you from this unpleasant situation as quickly as possible," I replied.

The lieutenant looked at me. "How? Bow Street thinks they have Theobald Jacombe's murderer. They aren't even looking for anyone else, I'd wager."

"Please do not use that term. Wagering is what got you into this mess," I reminded him. "Instead, tell me what happened last night."

"As you may have seen, my grandfather came to see me at Vauxhall. He'd learned about the duel, don't ask me how. He read me a lecture right in front of Molly on the mistakes I was making. He insulted her and me."

I remembered the old man's disdain for his grandson. "And then?"

"I took Molly to get something to eat, but the supper boxes were crowded. Instead, we went behind the Cascade, where I thought we could be private. We don't often get to be alone, you know."

"I understand."

The lieutenant drew a deep breath. "There was no one around except the drunken operator of the Cascade. I kept

Molly in the shadows away from view. She tried to persuade me to withdraw from the duel. Of course, I wasn't going to agree to that, so I kissed her."

"Er, a useful tactic," I murmured.

He gave a half smile. "Yes." He rubbed his square jaw. "Then everything seemed to happen at once. We heard a popping noise. A figure darted past us in the darkness. I couldn't tell whether it was a man or a woman."

"Are you certain you could not say whether it was a man or a woman?"

He shook his head. "Between the darkness and the quick way the figure went by, it was impossible."

"Very well."

"I started to lead Molly to the front of the Cascade, but then our attention was caught by the sight of a body in the back of the waterfall. I remember thinking to myself, who is that, and what has happened? Anxious to remove us from the situation, I turned Molly away from the scene, only to step on something hard in the grass. The gun. I picked it up without thinking."

He looked to me with an imploring expression on his angular features. I said, "I probably would have done the same thing in your situation. One does not like to see a pistol lying about. Rather unseemly."

The lieutenant's face cleared. "The gun was warm to the touch. I told Molly we should turn it over to one of the constables, but then, from nowhere, Mr. Lavender was on me. And some other fellow, finely dressed, was there as well."

"That would have been my valet, Robinson," I told him grimly.

"Your valet?" the lieutenant asked in surprise.

"The world is full of unbelievable coincidences. Now, Lieutenant, you do not remember anything else? Especially about the figure you saw run past you?"

The young man shook his head. "I've tried. It's hopeless. Everything was so dark. It was but a mere ghost of a human."

I suppressed a sigh. There was no doubt in my mind that Lieutenant Nevill spoke the truth. His account of the night's events matched Molly's if I needed any further evidence of his innocence. They had not had time to compare their stories. I felt deeply that the young soldier's honour was unquestionable. Besides, he reminded me a bit of myself at that age.

"What happened next, when you were brought to the Bow Street office?" I asked.

"Not much. I was told I would be held on suspicion of murdering Theobald Jacombe. My commander in the army released me from my duties so that Bow Street could bring me here."

This last was said with such an air of defeat, I felt a wave of pity for the lieutenant. Not even his commanding officer had stopped to question Bow Street or defend the soldier's reputation. "Your immediate discomfort has been eased a bit, but we must get you out of here. What about your grandfather? Can you appeal to him? Surely he could use his influence to have you released."

"I can't ask him."

"Why? Do not tell me your pride is standing in the way."

"He wouldn't help me anyway. He neither likes me nor approves of me."

"That cannot be so."

"It is."

I heard the sound of the guard unlocking the door. "Give me his direction. I shall go to him."

9

Mr. Nevill kept a set of meager rooms in South Audley Street. Upon my arrival, the old man opened the door himself. I wondered at his lack of a manservant.

"Who did you say you are?" he asked, his face pinched in concentration.

"Beau Brummell, a friend of your grandson's."

The door creaked open on its hinges. The old man, wrapped in a heavy brocade robe over his clothes, motioned with one knarled hand for me to enter. "This is about Nicky, eh? Sit down in that chair where I can see you. My eyes are not what they used to be."

I did as he asked, taking in the sparse furnishings, the lack of ornamentation on the walls. Mr. Nevill was known to be a man of wealth. Apparently, he disliked parting with a shilling of it.

"Mr. Nevill, are you aware that your grandson is being held at King's Bench Prison on suspicion of murdering Theobald Jacombe?"

"I said I could not see well. I did not say I was deaf and dumb," he chided me in his raspy voice.

I began to comprehend why the young lieutenant felt he would get no help from his grandfather. "Sir, the boy is innocent, as I'm sure you will agree."

"I am not agreeing to anything at the moment. The boy has too much feeling in him. Passion will be a man's downfall, you know."

How I wished for a glass of wine. "The lieutenant loves Molly, that is true. But he is also a man of honour who would never resort to cold-blooded murder. He was to fight a duel."

The old man snorted, then succumbed to a fit of coughing. "Just like his father, he is. Throwing himself away on a heartless flirt, a lightskirt to boot. You would think the boy would have learned, but he has not."

"What, er, happened to his father?"

Mr. Nevill's face seemed to crumple at the mention of his son. "Harry fell victim to the scheming ways of a jade named Arabella. She was a merchant's daughter, out for conquests. My Harry was helpless when she turned her calculating gaze on him. Thought she could get her hands on my money. He married her against my wishes. I settled some money on him, but told him there would be no more. She went through what I had given him, and the fortune he made in the East India Company, then eventually took off for the Continent with one of her lovers."

"Leaving him with a son, I take it."

He nodded, a miserable expression on his face. "Nicky was fourteen. Within a year of Arabella's leaving, Harry drank himself to death over her. Passions, too many passions will kill a man one way or another. Men should be strong, above such things. Now Nicky is repeating his father's mistake."

I thought about how the lieutenant had lost his father when he was fifteen, the same age as I had lost mine. "But, sir, you cannot know that Molly will play him false."

"Bah! Of course she will. One only has to look at her."

Look at a wholesome, pretty girl of seventeen years and think her a lightskirt?

"She might not have a chance to prove herself faithful. Unless someone steps forward to assist the lieutenant, he will be tried for Theobald Jacombe's murder. He might end up with his neck in a noose." That should get the old man's attention.

"He will go through the proper English court system. They will not convict him. There were no witnesses who saw the actual killing."

I sat appalled at this callous acceptance of his grandson's future of a trial where his life would be at stake. I looked into Mr. Nevill's cloudy eyes. "But, sir, will you not step forward in his defense? Your support right now is vital. All London is crying for justice in Jacombe's murder. Unless his own grandfather defends him, sees that he is released on bail into your charge, what chance does he have?"

"No, I shall not say a word on his behalf nor expend a shilling. He defied me with that hoyden, Molly. Now he must suffer the consequences," was the stubborn response.

"You do not believe for a minute that he pulled the trigger, do you?"

The old man's mouth worked. "It does not matter what I believe."

I rose, tension in every muscle of my body. Mr. Nevill's cold view of his grandson's predicament chilled me to the bone. That he should so reject the young soldier was incomprehensible to me.

Yet again I was thrown back in time to my relationship with my own unemotional father. I could feel his disapproval making me feel smaller and smaller. Mr. Nevill had the same lack of compassion for his grandson that my father had had for me. Though it was true Mr. Nevill did not believe the young man would be convicted.

I wanted to tell Mr. Nevill exactly how I felt about his heartless treatment of the young soldier, but I could not close the door on questioning him again if need be. Instead, I thanked him for his time and took my leave.

Walking back to Bruton Street in the sunlight, I felt a strong measure of pity for the lieutenant. His father had killed himself over a woman. His grandfather was punishing him for the sins of his father and the possibility that he might commit the same folly.

I was not happy when I entered my house. Sounds of a squealing pig met my ears when I put my walking stick in a silver container near the door.

Robinson appeared from his quarters near the kitchens. The expression on his face was thunderous. But I had neither the time nor the inclination to listen to his complaints.

"Robinson, have you thought any more about last night's events?"

He accepted my hat and gloves. "Yes, sir, I have. I am sorry to tell you that nothing new has come to my mind. Of course, I cannot think properly with that pig in the house."

"Are you certain you saw no one else behind that Cascade?"

"That I am sure of. It was terribly dark, sir. No, I cannot

say that I saw anyone other than the soldier, his ladyfriend, and the drunken operator of the Cascade."

"I am certain Bow Street questioned the operator. If he saw anyone, I would have heard about it, I expect. Still, perhaps I shall pay a call on Miss Lavender and see if her father has dropped any word."

"Is there any hope for the lieutenant?" Robinson asked.

"Not when even his grandfather refuses to lift a hand to help him. I shall have to create hope by finding out who else wished to see Theobald Jacombe dead."

"In the meantime, sir, a missive arrived from the Prince of Wales."

"Oh? Let me have it."

Robinson moved toward a table in the hall and picked up a crested, folded piece of vellum and handed it to me. "Also, this latest addition of *The General Evening Post* just arrived. You might want to look at the front page."

I took the newspaper from his hands. On the front page, the following appeared:

MURDER AT VAUXHALL
PLEASURE GARDENS

Lieutenant Nicholas Nevill, aged 20, is being held at King's Bench Prison on suspicion of murder in last night's grisly death of the highly respected and honoured Mr. Theobald Jacombe, aged 42. Sources report that Lieutenant Nevill had challenged Mr. Jacombe to a duel after a card game at London's notorious new gaming club, Watier's. Forced to defend his honour, Mr. Jacombe was said to have agreed to meet the lieutenant this morning. Instead, at last evening's gala event at Vauxhall Plea-

sure Gardens, which was under the patronage of His Royal Highness the Prince Wales, Mr. Jacombe was shot through the heart. His dead body caught in the mechanism of the Cascade exhibition and stunned onlookers when its lifeless form appeared in the waterfall. Bow Street is said to have found Lieutenant Nevill behind the Cascade with a pistol in his hand. A witness also saw the Lieutenant in this telling position. Funeral services for Mr. Jacombe, who is survived by his wife, will take place Thursday, 9 July, at 10 of the clock at St. George's Church, Hanover Square. It is expected that attendance will be high as Londoners come out to express their grief and outrage at this heinous crime.

"Good God, the lieutenant has already been tried and convicted in the public eye," I said.

"Things look very dark," replied Robinson.

I broke the seal on the Prince's note. All it said was for me to present myself immediately at Carlton House.

❦ 10 ❦

Carlton House, Pall Mall, had been given by King George III to his son for his use as long as he kept up the house and gardens and paid the taxes.

You may recall my telling you about Prinny's palace by the sea in Brighton during another of my adventures. If so, you know that Prinny loves to redesign and decorate buildings in the most costly of manners.

His current residence is certainly no exception. I barely had time to appreciate its beauty, no less nod a greeting to Petersham, Tallarico, and my friend Lord Perry, before Prinny motioned me into an ante-room furnished with expensive pieces from France.

"Brummell, what's to be done in this situation with Jacombe's death? All London is on its ear," he said.

"Er, to be done, sir? What do you mean?"

"You know what I mean. That soldier couldn't have killed Jacombe. You agree with me, don't you?"

"Yes, sir."

"Then do something about it. I can't have one of my troops hanged for a murder he didn't commit."

"It would not look good for you," I said, but the Prince missed my sarcasm.

"No, it wouldn't. Besides which, I don't like that such a horrifying event took place during an evening where I was host. That wouldn't look good for me either. Whoever did this is common, I tell you, no courageous soldier."

"Yes, sir. I confess that I have begun a bit of an investigation of my own—"

"Capital! Exactly what I wanted to hear. Keep me informed of your progress."

"The lieutenant is being held at King's Bench Prison," I said before he could move away. "Could you use your influence to have him released until the trial?"

"Me? Zeus! I can't get involved," the Prince said.

Just then, the door to the room we were in opened. At first I thought a breeze had swung it forward. Then I realised this was a short-sighted view on my part. John, Count Boruwlaski, the dwarf, entered the room and tugged on the tails of Prinny's coat, very like a child.

"We miss you in the Music Room, sir. Come sing for us," the Count implored in his high-pitched voice. "I'll stand on the pianoforte bench and turn the pages for Lord Perry to play while you sing."

Unwilling to witness such a scene, I took my leave and went home in a thoughtful mood.

Chakkri was lying in the exact centre of my bed when I arrived, one brown velvet paw flung over his eyes.

My last thoughts that night before falling asleep were of Lieutenant Nevill alone in his cell. While I could only be happy that he was alone and not suffering at the hands of his fellow inmates, I felt a rising apprehension at the swiftness at which matters were progressing.

Would I be able to find anyone else in London who would want to see Theobald Jacombe dead before the hangman's noose claimed the life of the young soldier?

Wednesday afternoon I decided to pay a call at the Haven of Hope. My purpose was twofold: I wanted to see Molly, to find out how she was getting on and whether or not she remembered anything new about the figure she and the lieutenant saw behind the Cascade. The figure of the murderer.

Secondly, I wished to see Miss Lavender, to determine whether I could elicit information from her as to Bow Street's findings. Specifically what her father knew about the operator of the Cascade.

This second task I was none too sure of accomplishing. Miss Lavender is careful to stay out of her father's dealings as much as possible. She can be quite tight-lipped when it comes to Bow Street matters.

The day was pleasantly warm with the sun shining, as I traveled in my sedan-chair to Covent Garden. Ned and Ted were in a cheerful mood, having breakfasted that morning on their mother's cooking. I expected that soon I would have to have a talk with André to make sure the French chef did not feel his territory invaded by the countrywoman.

Telling Ned and Ted to wait outside the Haven of Hope, I knocked on the door to the shelter.

Lionel opened the door to me. "Mr. Brummell, sir. Come on in."

"Glad of some male company, are you, Lion?"

He chuckled. "That's for sure. Bein' round females all the time makes my 'ead ache sometimes."

"Where are Molly and Miss Lavender?"

"Back in the kitchens. I'll let 'em know yer 'ere."

"No, I shall not disturb their work by having them entertain me in the sitting room. Are the other girls at their lessons?"

"Yes. That's where I'm supposed to be, too."

"Well, you had better go then. You would not want Miss Lavender to be cross with you."

"Before I go, there's one thing," Lionel said hesitantly.

I was immediately alert to the change in his mood. "And what is that, Lion?"

"It's Miss Lavender. She's not been 'erself since what 'appened at the Cascade."

"In what way?"

Lionel scratched his head. "It's 'ard to say. She just seems quiet and far-away like. When she does talk, it's all about the murder of that Jacombe fella'."

"Hmmm. I shall see what I can find out. Thank you for telling me."

"I don't like seein' her this way."

"Nor do I. Try not to worry yourself over it."

I saw Lionel into the room in front of the house where the girls took their lessons. I considered the boy's words, remembering how Miss Lavender had indeed behaved in a manner quite unlike herself that night at Vauxhall. But who among us could be themselves had they just witnessed a dead body coming over a waterfall?

I wandered to the back of the house and found myself standing in a modest kitchen, watching Miss Lavender peel carrots for her special stew I imagined. Molly was kneading bread dough. This domestic scene was marred only by the talk of murder.

"Mr. Brummell, have you seen Nicky?" Molly asked upon seeing me enter.

"Yes, I have. He has his own private cell now and is doing as well as can be expected under the circumstances."

"A private cell? How could he pay—Oh, you must have done that for him, Mr. Brummell! Thank you," Molly said.

Miss Lavender glanced up from the carrots. Today she wore a blue cotton gown, her dark red hair tied into a severe knot on the top of her head. "That was good of you, Mr. Brummell. That poor young man should not be made to suffer for a crime he didn't commit."

"I did what I could, but I want to do more. Molly, did you go to Bow Street this morning to give your statement?"

"Yes."

"Were you able to find out anything more?"

"Not a thing," she said, putting the bread into a baking tin. "That Mr. Read was there, as well as Miss Lavender's father. I told them what happened, over and over. They kept acting like there was something I wasn't saying, but there wasn't."

"I can imagine," I said.

Molly turned her almond-shaped dark eyes on me. "What's going to happen to Nicky, Mr. Brummell? How are we going to get him out of prison?"

"We must find someone else who wanted Mr. Jacombe dead," I told her.

The knife Miss Lavender had been using to slice the carrots fell to the kitchen floor with a clatter.

"You did not cut yourself, did you?" I asked in concern.

"No, I am just clumsy today, it seems," Miss Lavender

said. Then she picked the knife up from the floor, put it in the sink, and got out a clean one. She resumed chopping the vegetables in a methodical fashion.

"As to having the lieutenant released from prison," I said, "I went to see his grandfather. The man was not very helpful, I am afraid."

"He's a bitter, unfeeling old man," Molly replied hotly. "He thinks only of his precious money."

"And of his lost son," I reminded her.

"It's all the same, isn't it? Mr. Nevill's son, Nicky's father, was involved in some banking deal that went bad. It almost cost old Mr. Nevill his fortune. Nicky told me all about it. His grandfather had to help his father, Mr. Nevill Junior, out of it. In fact, I forgot all about this before, but I'm pretty sure Mr. Jacombe was involved somehow."

"Mr. Jacombe?" I said, instantly alert.

Molly narrowed her eyes in concentration. "Yes. Yesterday at the prison, Nicky told me that the only time he'd even heard the name 'Jacombe,' before he met the man at your club, was in a conversation he overheard between his father and his grandfather years ago. He thought it may not have even been the same Jacombe. At any rate, it all had to do with a bank Mr. Jacombe was operating at the time. This was all years ago. That's all I know."

"I wish I had known this before I went to see Mr. Nevill. It might be important. But no matter. I shall find out more about it."

Molly shrugged. "I don't see how it can matter now. Miss Lavender, I've finished with the bread. Can I go see Nicky?"

"Sure you may," Miss Lavender said with a faint smile.

Molly took off her apron, thanked me for my help with

the lieutenant, and hurried from the room, leaving Miss Lavender and me alone.

"Miss Lavender, how are you today?"

"I'm fine," she said. "Anxious about the lieutenant, like everyone else."

I sensed there was more going on than worry over the lieutenant, but I could not put my finger on what it was. "I wonder what Bow Street found out about the operator of the Cascade." I threw this out, not expecting the investigator's daughter to share any Bow Street secrets.

"Seamus O'Toole. A known drunk. He didn't see or hear anything, including the gunshot, he was in such a drink-induced fog. Father had to bring him round to consciousness when he found the lieutenant holding the gun. O'Toole's been employed at Vauxhall for two years and hasn't caused any trouble, despite his propensity for drink. Apparently he has his drinking timed well so he can still perform his duties before becoming oblivious."

I stood stunned. Miss Lavender never reveals anything in regard to her father's work. Yet here she was, telling me everything her father had apparently shared with her. Even her desire to see Lieutenant Nevill freed would not normally induce her to talk about Bow Street matters. Why was she so forthcoming now? Not that I am complaining, mind you.

She chattered on. "Father says he and Mr. Read are sorry for the young soldier, but believe him guilty. Both Father and your man, Robinson, saw the lieutenant holding the murder weapon. The gun was a common pocket pistol of no particular distinction, so worn that the maker's name was illegible."

"The kind that could be purchased anywhere."

"Yes. But Bow Street thinks the lieutenant is the one,

and that he acted out of passion. I tried to talk to Father, but he won't listen to me, and it just turned into a big argument. Mr. Brummell, we have to do something to help Lieutenant Nevill. What is your next move?"

We?

She argued with her father over the case?

She wanted to help me in the investigation?

"Well, Miss Lavender, I own I am grateful for your help. I cannot think what to do, other than find out as much as possible about Theobald Jacombe in hopes that we might uncover an enemy."

Miss Lavender studied the carrots intently. "Perhaps he had several enemies."

"All the better. But who were they? Were they at Vauxhall Monday night? We need facts."

She looked up at me, a flicker of light in her green eyes. "What can I do? I don't believe the lieutenant killed Jacombe, and I must learn who did. I must know."

I stared at her. What was going on here? Why was Miss Lavender suddenly not content to let her father handle Bow Street work? Why was she so passionate about finding out who the killer was? Was it all to do with Molly and the lieutenant, or was something else going on here?

Behind us in the hall, the door to the teaching-room opened and girls spilled out, laughing and talking. There was no further opportunity for conversation.

Reluctantly, I left the Haven of Hope, but not before noting the deep circles under Miss Lavender's eyes and the way her hands shook as she rubbed them clean on her apron.

✺ 11 ✺

On my way to the Jacombe residence, I thought of Miss Lavender's peculiar behaviour. First at Vauxhall, now at her shelter. Clearly the murder had affected my friend deeply. But why? From the time she had overheard Mr. Nevill talk about her shelter—and the mention of Mr. Jacombe's name, I suddenly realised—through the ugly scene at Vauxhall and now at her shelter, Miss Lavender had not behaved like herself. She is a strong, independent woman, yet in the face of these events, she had become withdrawn. Now she seemed almost obsessed with the killing. Even Lion had noticed.

I needed more time to draw her out, but right now, I wanted to pay a call on the new widow.

The Jacombes' house off Portman Square was distinguishable by the black hatchment over the door. When I knocked, the portal was opened by a butler wearing a black armband. After giving him my card and asking for the mistress of the house, I was taken past a gleaming hall and into a pristine sitting-room. This room was reserved, I presumed, for guests waiting to be shown abovestairs to the drawing room.

I admired the green-and-ivory-decorated room, which contained lovely pieces of furniture in the Chippendale style. Two green-and-ivory-striped chairs faced a green sofa. Oil paintings and a large gilt-framed mirror graced the walls. By the empty fireplace, pots of flowers stood.

The door opened after a few minutes, and a woman entered. My first thought was that she was not Mrs. Jacombe, and that I knew her from somewhere. I could not think where. She was a woman of average height and very neat. Everything from her heavy black bombazine gown, with its ring of keys worn on a cord about her waist, to her plain brown hair dusted with grey, labeled her as housekeeper.

Perhaps that was why she seemed familiar. Because she looked like dozens of housekeepers I had seen before.

"Mr. Brummell, how good of you to call. I am Mrs. Hargrove, the housekeeper," she said in measured tones.

She would be the type to know exactly who I was and what my position in Society was. It was her business to know members of Society and of the merchant class. One look into her cold brown eyes, and that one sentence spoken, told me I was dealing with an efficient woman whose entire life revolved around this household.

"Thank you, Mrs. Hargrove," I returned. "Is Mrs. Jacombe receiving?"

"I am afraid not. She is resting in preparation for tomorrow's funeral and cannot be disturbed." This was said in a calm tone, but one that clearly indicated that contesting her words would be futile.

"I understand. Please be so good as to let her know that I called." I made as if to leave the room.

"Would you like me to inform her Royal Highness, the Duchess of York, that you are here?"

Freddie? Here at the Jacombes'? I looked again at Mrs. Hargrove and marveled at the extent of her knowledge of the people in Society. "Yes, please do. I did not know she was visiting."

"The Royal Duchess is an acquaintance of Mrs. Jacombe's. I shall just be a minute. Would you care for a glass of wine while you wait?"

"Yes, thank you."

How did she know?

Mrs. Hargrove served me a full glass of excellent burgundy before leaving the room without a sound. Some ten minutes passed—more than enough time for me to finish the wine—then Freddie appeared in the doorway, dressed in a somber, dove-coloured gown.

"George! I did not realise you knew Lady Venetia."

I bowed low. "Freddie, what are you doing here, and who is Lady Venetia?"

She sat down on the green sofa and indicated a place next to her. Nothing could have kept me from it. I gazed into her china-blue eyes, hoping to see a return of the warmth I could once detect there. Alas, while her expression was cordial, that invisible wall still remained.

"Lady Venetia is Mrs. Jacombe. She comes from Weybridge originally, and I knew her father a little. I call on her most times when I come to London."

Weybridge is the county where Freddie lives.

"She is a titled lady, then?"

"Yes, the daughter of an earl, long deceased. I should not call her Lady Venetia, as she chose to be known instead as simply Mrs. Jacombe out of respect for her husband when they married."

"A touch unusual," I mused. So Jacombe had married into the peerage. That could only have served to add to his consequence during his climb up the governmental ladder.

"It was a love match. They have been married for eighteen years. Lady Venetia is in quite a state since her husband's murder. I came directly to her as soon as the Duke told me Mr. Jacombe had been killed over by the Cascade, and I have stayed here ever since."

"That is good of you, Freddie. I take it Mrs. Jacombe is completely overset by her husband's death."

"Indeed, George. She has always been of a delicate constitution. This has her all to pieces. Her physician, Doctor Trusdale, is attending her."

"That bad, is it?"

"Dreadful, really. I have not seen Lady Venetia ever so distressed, as I expect is normal given the circumstances. We only just got her to take some broth this morning, George."

At that moment, a greyhound pranced into the room.

"Oh, dear," Freddie exclaimed. "I do not know what Gabriel can be doing downstairs. Come on," she called to the dog.

The greyhound looked at her worshipfully, as all dogs are prone to do.

Some humans as well. Ahem.

"Will you be at the Perrys' house this evening, Freddie? A dinner party would not be inappropriate."

About to exit the room with the dog, Freddie glanced at me over her shoulder. "I do not think so. Lady Venetia needs me."

I reluctantly took my leave, mulling over the fact that Mr. Jacombe had married above his station in life. If it had been a love match, had the love on Mr. Jacombe's part been of Lady Venetia's rank?

❧ 12 ❧

Not until the following day at St. George's Church did I get my first glimpse of Mrs. Jacombe.

The church was crowded with people, but it was not difficult to pick out the widow. Her small, slim figure hardly seemed strong enough to hold up the yards of material of her heavy black silk dress and veil.

Still, she was quite beautiful with her dark hair, large hazel eyes, and small mouth, but there was an air of sadness about her that went beyond the accoutrements of mourning.

Beside her, a tall, thin, dark-haired man with stern features guided her gently down the aisle to the front pew. I wondered if this was Doctor Trusdale, her physician. Freddie and the Duke accompanied them.

"Don't stand there gaping, George, come and sit with me. James is home with a putrid throat," a gruff voice spoke.

I turned to see my good friend, the Marchioness of Salisbury, at my side. A tiny but sturdy lady in her fifties, the marchioness is known for her unladylike skills on the hunting field. She is outspoken, blunt, and was Prinny's mistress when he was twenty and she was past thirty.

I executed a bow. "My lady, you are most kind."

"No, I'm not. I just want someone to gossip with about all these people, and you'll do. Have you ever seen the like over a plain mister?"

"All the world seems to be here," I answered as we seated ourselves.

The service was long. Many of Mr. Jacombe's government cronies spoke at length of his good qualities and fine skills in making Bow Street what it is today. Even Earl Spencer stood up and said a few words on behalf of his friend.

Next to me, I could tell Lady Salisbury was fidgeting in her seat like a girl of ten summers.

When it was over, she said, "How boring this Jacombe man sounds. I didn't know him myself, but James said that since he couldn't attend, I should come in his place. Something about respect for Earl Spencer. Hmpf. Is it true what's going around regarding a duel?"

"Yes. Mr. Jacombe The Pious was cheating at cards in my club the night he was murdered."

Lady Salisbury's face lit up. "Oh, tell me everything."

"I wish I knew everything, my lady. This Mr. Jacombe is so very highly regarded, yet I know he tried to slip a king of diamonds into a deck of cards in play with a young soldier."

"Lieutenant Nevill?"

"You have been following the newspapers."

"Who hasn't, George? This is the biggest scandal London's seen since Prinny tried to divorce his wife."

"Yes, it was Lieutenant Nevill. I believed his accusation that Jacombe had been cheating, yet I tried to keep matters from escalating to the point of a duel. I failed when the situation became more personal, so I determined to be the lieutenant's second."

"You're an honourable man, George, I'll give you that."

"My lady, the happiness you bring me by saying so—"

"Hah," she barked. "What else do you know?"

"Not much, other than that the lieutenant is innocent."

"Is he? Then Bow Street is preparing a case to hang the wrong man."

"Indeed. If only I knew more about Jacombe. Perhaps I could find an enemy who wanted to see him dead. Everyone here seems so genuinely grieved over his passing."

Almost to mock my words, at that moment a trill of laughter sounded from an expensively dressed brunette on the arm of the Earl of Fogingham, or "Foggie" as he is known, due to his love of drink and the perpetual drunken haze he lives in.

"That's Mrs. Roucliffe, a popular courtesan," Lady Salisbury informed me. "Trust Foggie to bring her to St. George's."

"You shock me. Ladies of your rank are not supposed to know such women exist."

"What a lot of rubbish! You just said you wanted to know more about Jacombe." Lady Salisbury inclined her head toward Mrs. Roucliffe. "There would be a place to start. Word is Jacombe tried to set her up as his mistress."

"No, Mr. Jacombe with a mistress?"

"Why not? She isn't a stunning beauty, but men like her. She must be good at her trade."

I smiled at this frank remark. "Lady Salisbury, will you marry me?"

She smiled back. "You may call on me when James is six feet under."

I confess I felt inappropriately lighthearted at that moment until I perceived that Miss Lavender, accompanied by her father, stood toward the back of the church.

Then I frowned. Even from a distance, I could tell Miss Lavender was extremely upset.

I escorted Lady Salisbury to the door, and observed Mrs. Hargrove, the Jacombe housekeeper, sitting quietly without a trace of emotion on her face in the last pew.

I then doubled back to see Miss Lavender. I noted that Mr. Nevill was slowly making his way to the door. I wanted to speak to him, so I made my conversation with Miss Lavender brief. "A sad day, it seems," I said.

"A great loss to Bow Street," came Mr. Lavender's reply.

Miss Lavender had that faraway look on her face, her skin almost translucent in the light of the church. Her gaze was fixed on the coffin draped in black at the front of the aisle near the pulpit.

"Miss Lavender," I said, "I must speak with someone now, but I wonder if I might take you and Lionel to Gunter's for ices later."

She dragged her gaze to me. "That would be lovely."

"Shall we say two hours' time? I shall bring a hackney coach to the Haven of Hope and collect you and the boy."

Mr. Lavender glared at me, his bushy brows coming together to form one hairy line of disapproval above his eyes. As usual in my presence.

Ever independent, Miss Lavender ignored him and said, "I should like that. Thank you."

I hastened away before Mr. Lavender could bellow a word and before old Mr. Nevill could leave the premises. As it was, I caught up with the latter outside, where a jumble of carriages and sedan-chairs awaited their masters.

"Mr. Nevill, may I have a word with you?"

Mr. Nevill looked at me with his cloudy eyes squinted against the sunlight. "Oh, it is Mr. Brummell, is it? What do you want?"

Not the best of beginnings. I decided to charge right in. "I understand that you and your son were involved in a banking adventure with the late Mr. Jacombe. One that went seriously awry and almost cost you everything."

I thought the old man would have an apoplexy right there. "How did you find out about that?" he demanded.

He himself had just confirmed what Molly said, but it would not do to let him know that. "Old scandals live on, you know."

"I told my son, Harry, not to get involved in that bank deal. But he was driven by his insatiable wife to make more and more money. He bought stock in a bank partially owned by Jacombe. They lent a great amount of money to the Prince and never got repaid."

I could believe that. Prinny was not one to look back when it came to money. "Your son had stock in that bank and was liable for the bank's debts."

"Of course he was. That is the way it works, you know."

"And the debts were called in?"

"Yes, they were, more's the pity. Stockholders had to come up with the money. I paid Harry's portion to prevent him and his family from being ruined and sent to debtor's prison."

"That was good of you. And Mr. Jacombe?"

"Jacombe had already sold his stock by the time the debts

were called in. The way his crafty lawyers had written the whole thing, no one could touch him."

"Did Jacombe know that the stock in the bank was worthless when he sold it to your son?"

The old man narrowed his eyes at me. "I am not sorry the bastard is dead if that is what you are getting at."

"So why did you come here today?"

"I always enjoy a good funeral, and the next one may be my own."

So saying, the cantankerous Mr. Nevill limped away on his cane, a footman rushing to guide his master to an ancient coach.

Did Mr. Nevill hate Jacombe enough over that banking deal to kill him all these years later? That did not make sense. I could more easily see him killing Jacombe to protect his grandson.

If he did kill him, perhaps he did so because he felt the end of his life was near and wanted to revenge himself and spare his grandson a duel before he died. Did he plan to turn himself in to Bow Street at some point? Was he allowing his grandson to be accused in the meantime as some sort of punishment for defying him? How cruel that would be.

And at what point would he step in and rescue the soldier from a hanging death?

❈ 13 ❈

Gunter's confectionery is best known for its delicious ices. The shop is also one of the few places a single lady can meet a gentleman without causing damage to her reputation.

I procured three strawberry ices and sat down with Miss Lavender and Lionel at a small table near the window overlooking Berkeley Square. The boy's eyes widened at the sight of the strawberry treat placed in front of him.

Miss Lavender picked up her spoon, but instead of eating, she addressed me. "What have you found out about Jacombe? Anything that might help us clear the lieutenant's name?"

"Mr. Jacombe's halo is beginning to look a bit tarnished," I remarked. "It seems he was not above shady business dealings."

Miss Lavender looked at me intently. "What do you mean?"

"He sold worthless bank stock to the lieutenant's father."

"That only makes the lieutenant look worse, doesn't it?" she asked, distress touching her words. "Wouldn't this be more motive for the lieutenant to kill Jacombe?"

"Not necessarily," I pointed out. "His grandfather is the one who bailed his son out of trouble. Old Mr. Nevill took a loss financially. He would actually be the one with more motive for revenge, especially when you consider that he is extremely tight-fisted with his money."

Lionel finished his ice and looked longingly at his plate.

"Would you like more?" I asked him.

The grin on his face gave me my answer. I signalled for another ice.

Lionel said, "I found out somethin' about that Jacombe fella'."

Both Miss Lavender and I turned startled gazes on the boy.

Miss Lavender said, "What did you find out?"

"Promise you won't get mad at me," he implored.

"Lionel, tell us at once what you learned," Miss Lavender said. "This is a serious situation. An innocent man has been accused of murder."

"I 'ad to do something with that foppish idiot Fairingdale pointin' at me and sayin' I might 'ave delivered some note to Jacombe."

"No one believes you did, Lionel," I said. "I am certain Bow Street is not even following up on the fact that a boy delivered a note."

"Mr. Brummell's right, Lionel," Miss Lavender said. "Bow Street knows there were hundreds of boys there that night. It would be impossible to find out which one the killer used to deliver the message."

I nodded. "Even if there were witnesses, they are sure to disagree. You have nothing to worry about."

Lionel shrugged. "Well, then, anyways, sometimes I slips out to see some o' my old friends down in Seven Dials. That's 'ow I found out what I did."

Miss Lavender bristled at the mention of the notorious slums. "You know I don't like you going there."

Lionel ducked his head. "But iffen I'm to be a Bow Street Runner, I'll be going there and to worse."

Miss Lavender drew a deep breath. There was no arguing with this logic.

Lionel continued. "Anyhow, I asked round about Jacombe. Seems it's known that Jacombe was the man with money in a bear-baitin' show."

"That's despicable!" Miss Lavender cried. "Those poor dogs used to agitate the pitiful bears to fight. The whole thing is cruel."

"I have never been one to enjoy the sport myself," I said, remembering the one time I had been witness to a bear-baiting.

The entire episode had struck me as uncivilized. I suppose I have a soft spot when it comes to animals, you know, especially when it comes to one particular Siamese cat.

Lionel received his second ice. Before he dug in, he said, "I think Jacombe made lots of money off the bear-baitin' scheme. It's said 'e 'ad a partner, some physician or such."

Doctor Trusdale? I wondered. Out loud I said, "I think Mr. Jacombe's character was not what everyone believes it to be, in fact—"

I interrupted myself at that moment. For Mrs. Roucliffe, the courtesan, whom, according to Lady Salisbury, Mr. Jacombe had been trying to set up as his mistress, had just walked into the shop. All eyes turned to her.

Again, it was not that she had a pretty face. Rather, there was something in the way she carried herself. She had a confident, seductive walk. Also, she wore a striking cherry-and-white-striped gown, cut very low across the bosom, revealing a great deal of flesh.

"Er, will you excuse me for a moment, please?" I said.

"Is there something wrong?" Miss Lavender asked.

"No, rather there is someone I must speak with," I told Miss Lavender and Lionel.

Miss Lavender looked over to where Mrs. Roucliffe stood and then back to me.

I could not fathom what the expression on her face meant.

"I shall return in a moment," I assured her.

I walked over to Mrs. Roucliffe. "I beg your pardon for addressing you without a proper introduction, Mrs. Roucliffe," I began, knowing she would not care two straws for the proprieties.

She turned and smiled at me. I saw in that smile the charm she held for men. For it lit up her rather plain countenance and made the receiver feel as if she thought him the most special of men.

"But I know who you are, Mr. Brummell, so there is no need to apologise," she said in a voice with a slight—false—French accent. I wondered what her real name was and where she came from. Probably Yorkshire or some other town right here in England.

"You are very kind, Mrs. Roucliffe. I wonder if I might impose upon that very kindness and beg an interview with you?"

She tilted her head and studied me. "Why, I would be delighted. Come to my house tomorrow at two," she said, extracting a peach-coloured card from her reticule and hand-ing it to me. I looked down to see her name and a direction on Half Moon Street.

"Thank you, I shall be there," I told her. I made her a little bow and turned back to the table where I had been sitting with Miss Lavender and Lionel, only to find it empty.

I looked around Gunter's, but they were gone. I hoped Miss Lavender was not out of temper with me. I could not see why she would be, but, I confess, the ways of females are sometimes foreign to me.

Can you imagine that? But there you are. It is the truth. I am not infallible, you know.

As for Miss Lavender, I had asked her to excuse me for a moment. Very unlike her to simply leave without speaking to me.

Walking out the door into the street, I saw Mr. Lavender standing there waiting for me. Could he have had anything to do with his daughter's abrupt departure?

"Well, laddie, explain yourself."

"Explain myself? What can you mean? And what are you doing here? Spying on me? Where did Miss Lavender go?"

The Bow Street investigator remained indignant. "She's gone back to the Haven of Hope, where she should be. I followed my daughter out of concern, concern I see was well-founded. There you were, exactly like a family, eating the ices and smiling at my daughter."

"She is lovely."

"I know that! I've told you before to stay away from her."

"I find I cannot."

"Have you considered the consequences of your actions?" he asked, his voice rising.

"Miss Lavender is quite slim. I doubt partaking of sweets

will put her figure in any danger," I replied, deliberately misunderstanding him.

He pointed a finger at me, a mannerism he employs when he is angry at me. "Don't play games with me. My daughter is a vulnerable lass. Have you thought that her affections might be engaged? Hard as it is to see why, but nevertheless, have you considered she might hold you in esteem?"

For some reason, I felt a glow at these words. During the length of my acquaintance with Miss Lavender, I had never considered that she might have finer feelings for me. The thought was not unpleasant. Not at all. Although, nor was it proper, I supposed.

As if he could read my mind, Mr. Lavender looked like a stack of fireworks ready to explode up into the sky. "Keep away from my daughter, I'm warning you, Mr. Brummell."

"Perhaps I might be distracted by investigating Mr. Jacombe's murder since Bow Street is not," I taunted him.

"Go right ahead, laddie. That's just the sort of pointless thing you would do, when we have the murderer in custody."

"Surely you do not believe Lieutenant Nevill is the type to commit such a cold-blooded act. He was to fight the man the next morning in an honourable way."

"That's exactly why he killed him. He knew he could never best Jacombe in that duel. Instead, he chose the cowardly way out."

"You are wrong. The cowardly way out would have been to simply not show his face at the appointed time of the duel."

"And not get his revenge for the slight on his lady and for the alleged cheating at cards? I don't think so. No, the lieutenant shot Mr. Jacombe, pure and simple."

"What about the person viewed running from the scene of the crime? What is your explanation for that? Have you tried to find him or her?"

"If there really was such a person, and we only have the lieutenant's and Molly's word for it, then likely it was someone who saw a murder take place and was frightened."

"Or it was the real killer."

"Ach! There is no sense talking to you. You have a way of twisting things around."

"Looking for the truth."

He had turned to go, but swung back to face me at those words. "I have the truth in the Jacombe murder. Go and meddle around if you like to stave off your boredom, but keep away from my daughter while you're doing it."

The Bow Street man stomped across the square, leaving me to my thoughts. I turned my steps toward Bruton Street, considering what Lionel had told me about Mr. Jacombe's involvement with bear-baiting.

It was not just that I considered the practice obscene and another chink in Mr. Jacombe's armour, it was the fact that Mr. Jacombe had some sort of business partnership with the physician. I was sure it had to be Doctor Trusdale. Tomorrow I would call again at the Jacombes' house and see if I could speak with the widow. If not, perhaps her physician would be in attendance, and I could question him.

I arrived home to find the house quiet.

Robinson appeared and greeted me. "Good afternoon, sir. Will you be changing for the evening soon?"

"In a few moments. I want to read my letters and invitations. How is everything, or should I ask?"

Robinson's lips pursed. "Ned and Ted took Mrs. Ed to

the greengrocers at Covent Garden. She is going to cook us mutton the way it should be prepared."

"I shall look forward to it," I lied.

Robinson handed me a small silver tray containing a stack of folded vellum. And a piece of straw.

I picked up the straw and held it between two fingers. "What is this?"

"Oh, I am sorry," Robinson said in a false tone. "Mrs. Ed brought straw into the house for her piglet. I do not know how that piece found its way onto this tray. I shall take it and dispose of it for you, sir."

Mentally, I heaved a weary sigh. Robinson had reached new heights with his Martyr Act. "I shall be in my book-room for the next half hour, then we will begin the evening's Dressing Hour."

"Very well, sir."

I poured myself a glass of wine and sat behind my desk. Immediately, Chakkri presented himself. He enjoys sitting on my desk, swishing his tail from side to side and generally creating havoc. His goal seems to be to knock the inkstand to the carpet. I opened an invitation to a merchant's party and scanned the lines with one hand while stroking Chakkri with the other.

"Well, old boy, it never ceases to amaze me that people I do not even know ask my attendance at their daughters' coming-out parties. Am I really so powerful? Do they think a nod from me will set their daughter on a course of marrying into the peerage?"

Chakkri muttered something unintelligible. It was almost a snort. I removed my hand from his back and reached for the rest of the mail. I flipped through various other cards of invitation and letters from friends.

Then I came to a letter that made me sit up in my chair and stare at the words on the fine paper. In a carefully printed hand were the following lines: *Find a way to free Lieutenant Nevill. He did not kill Mr. Jacombe. I know because I did.*

❧ 14 ❧

The words in the message from the killer haunted me
throughout an otherwise pleasant—if you did not count all
the talk of Mr. Jacombe's murder—dinner party at Lord
Perry's Grosvenor Square Town house. The very idea that
the killer himself knew I was looking into the murder
chilled me.

I could not decide whether to show the letter to Mr.
Lavender. Would he confiscate it? Scoff at it, saying it was
of my own invention?

I judged the latter to be the more likely scenario.
Therefore, I would keep it to myself. A plan formed in my
mind of trying to get samples of handwriting from the suspects in the case. The problem was, I had only one real
suspect, other than the lieutenant, and that was his grandfather.

Thus far, the old man was the only person I considered
who might have the motive and opportunity to put a period
to Mr. Jacombe's life.

Not only did he have the history of that disastrous banking deal, but another thought occurred to me. Perhaps the harsh exteriour Mr. Nevill presented did not run all the way through the man. Perhaps he had been the one to kill Mr. Jacombe, fearing the man would slaughter his grandson in the upcoming duel. Perhaps in his mind, Lieutenant Nevill's having to spend some time in gaol was a small price to pay for his life.

These thoughts were interrupted when I perceived that Freddie had entered the room on the arm of Victor Tallarico, who was clad in his usual choice of pink waistcoat.

Here was a surprise. I thought Freddie had told me she would not be attending the Perrys' party this evening. The Italian must have changed her mind. How vexing that he would have that sort of influence over her, do you not agree?

I bowed low to her. "Good evening, your Royal Highness. I am happy you are here. I dared not hope to see you after your words this afternoon."

"Good evening, George."

Tallarico flashed me his grin, the one that charms females of any age. "The *bellina duchessa* needed an evening among friends."

"Your Royal Highness, you know I would have escorted you," I said, ignoring the Italian.

"George, Victor just persuaded me to join him a short time ago. I did not like to leave Lady Venetia, but Mrs. Hargrove assured me she would take care of her."

"Mrs. Hargrove reminds me of someone I know," I mused.

"I cannot think who," Freddie said.

Neither could I. "Do you think Mrs. Jacombe would be

willing to receive me tomorrow? I would like to question her about her husband."

"Oh, George, only if you are very careful. She is so fragile, you know."

"I promise."

"Then come in the late morning or early afternoon. She is at her best then, before the day grows long and her thoughts become more agitated."

After agreeing that I would present myself at the Jacombe house no later than one, I was forced to go in with the rest of the party to the dining room.

I frowned when I found out I was seated too far away from Freddie—who was already sitting next to Tallarico— to converse with her. Soon after the uneventful dinner was over, I took my leave.

A quick look-in at White's, and later at Watier's, confirmed what I already knew: All of London wanted to see Lieutenant Nevill hanged for the murder of Mr. Jacombe. Not only did they want this to happen, but they were, in fact, growing more and more impatient for it. The words I heard chilled me.

"What's taking Bow Street so long?"

"They should turn the matter over to the Lord Chief Justice and be done with it."

"He'll see that the cowardly soldier meets his end. At the end of a rope!"

All this was the talk in the clubs, repeated in various forms throughout the evening. Bets were even recorded at White's Club as to the length of time the lieutenant would breathe after the hangman's noose broke his neck.

How long would it be before the young soldier was tried and convicted and the inevitable sentence carried out? I found myself filled with a sense of urgency to find the author of that note and make him or her held accountable for Mr. Jacombe's murder so Lieutenant Nevill could be freed.

True to my word, I presented myself at the Jacombe house the next day at one. This time, the butler showed me directly upstairs to a darkened sitting room.

On a blue-and-silver-striped sofa, Mrs. Jacombe's small frame rested. Within easy reach stood a round table of Chippendale's making, littered with bottles of medicines. Her greyhound lay curled at her feet. Mrs. Jacombe wore a black silk dress with a high neck. Her beauty was marred by dark circles under her eyes and, again, that air of sadness hung over her like a cloud of gloom.

Freddie sat nearby in a blue chair, her lovely features fixed in an expression of concern for her friend. She rose when I entered the room, the skirts of her lavender dress rustling, and performed the introductions.

"Thank you for receiving me, Mrs. Jacombe," I said, making her a small bow.

"You are most welcome, Mr. Brummell. Frederica speaks highly of you." She extended a hand to the table, her eyes scanning the bottles of medicine. Finally, she selected one. Removing the stopper from the bottle, she placed three drops of the potion into a glass of wine and began sipping the contents. "I am sorry. Where are my manners? Let me ring for Mrs. Hargrove to bring you some wine. Or would you prefer tea?"

"Wine would be delightful," I said, sitting in the chair she indicated next to Freddie.

Mrs. Jacombe rang a small bell placed on the table. Mrs.

Hargrove entered the room silently. The request for refreshment was put to her, and before the space of two minutes went by, I found a glass in my hand.

I smiled my thanks at Mrs. Hargrove, but she did not return the smile. Instead, her usual unemotional mask was in place. My brain worked trying to remember where I had seen her before, for I could not shake the feeling that I knew her.

We chatted of the weather for a few minutes, then I said, "Mrs. Jacombe, you are fortunate to have such an efficient housekeeper."

"She is a treasure," Mrs. Jacombe sighed. "Of course, there was that sorrow long ago. I do not believe Mrs. Hargrove ever quite recovered from it."

About to open my mouth and question what it was she meant, I was pleased when Freddie did the asking for me. "What was that, Lady Venetia?"

"A terrible thing, really, but Mr. Jacombe handled it all so well." Mrs. Jacombe took another sip of her medicated wine. Then, "A child. Mrs. Hargrove found herself with child not long after we employed her. I thought certainly we must dismiss her, but Mr. Jacombe insisted we should not. Naturally, after the baby was born, arrangements were made for it to be taken care of by a couple, and Mrs. Hargrove resumed her duties."

"How sad," Freddie said.

"It was charitable of you and Mr. Jacombe to be so kind to Mrs. Hargrove," I said. And it was true. Ordinarily, when a servant became pregnant, she was tossed out to fend for herself, sometimes even without a reference.

Tears came to Mrs. Jacombe's eyes. She picked up a black-edged handkerchief and wiped the moisture away. "Please forgive me. I cry quickly these past few days."

"That is understandable," I said. I felt sorry for Mrs. Jacombe. No merry widow was she. Apparently it had been a love-match, as Freddie had told me.

Just then the tall, thin, dark-haired man who had supported Mrs. Jacombe at the funeral walked into the room.

"Mrs. Jacombe, are you overexerting yourself?" he asked with an arch look in my direction. He seemed the sort who would not hesitate to order me from the room if he thought me interfering with the well-being of his patient.

"No, Doctor Trusdale, I am fine, really," she replied, looking pale. "Let me make you known to Mr. Brummell. Mr. Brummell, this is Doctor Trusdale. He has been our family physician since Mr. Jacombe and I married eighteen years ago."

I stood and extended my hand to the physician. He took it and gave it a brief, firm shake. He was a good-looking man, probably in his mid-forties, but wearing his years well. His attention did not remain on me for long. Instead, he went directly to Mrs. Jacombe and gently held her wrist while taking out a pocketwatch and timing her pulse. The greyhound jumped down and ambled out of the room.

"Did you sleep well last night?" Doctor Trusdale asked her.

"I am afraid not," Mrs. Jacombe said.

"Did you try the new mixture of laudanum?"

"Yes," Mrs. Jacombe responded weakly. Tears formed in her eyes again and slowly fell down her pale cheeks. "It is no good, I am afraid. Nothing can ease my pain."

The physician turned and looked at me, but I did not need a hint from him to know it was time to take my leave.

Freddie moved her chair closer to Mrs. Jacombe and mur-

mured comforting words. Doctor Trusdale was busy check-
ing the bottles of medicine.

I slipped from the room with a soft goodbye, and walked
down the stairs in a somber mood.

In the hallway, Mrs. Hargrove was petting the greyhound. "Gabriel," I recalled, was his name. She had a treat
for him and made him stand on his hind legs to receive it.
When he obeyed, a rare smile tilted Mrs. Hargrove's lips.

A smile that reached her almond-shaped brown eyes.

That was when I knew. Another pair of almond-shaped
brown eyes flashed in my mind.

Molly's.

It was Molly whom Mrs. Hargrove reminded me of. I
looked closer. Yes, the shape of the eyes and the shape of
the face were exactly the same. Something about the nose as
well. The resemblance was uncanny.

Everything came together in my mind. Molly did not
know who her parents were. Mrs. Hargrove gave birth soon
after coming to work for the newly married Jacombe couple.
That would make the child seventeen years old. Exactly
Molly's age.

"Is there something I can help you with, Mr. Brummell?"
Mrs. Hargrove inquired.

I realised I had been staring at the housekeeper. "No, I
shall be on my way."

She eyed me with a hint of suspicion quickly masked.

I exited the house and entered my sedan-chair. Ned and
Ted carried me to Half Moon Street, where I would inter-
view Mrs. Roucliffe, but my mind was on the housekeeper.
Which brought me to a question: Who was Molly's father?
The idea that it might well be Mr. Jacombe himself burst
in my brain. My mind went back to the heated words be-

tween Lieutenant Nevill and Mr. Jacombe at Watier's that fateful night. I remembered that when the soldier had declared his love for Molly, the first question Mr. Jacombe had asked had been, "Who is her father?" Was this significant? Had Mr. Jacombe kept the pregnant housekeeper, knowing that if he threw her out on the streets, she would tell his new bride that the child was his? It would not be the first time such a scene in fashionable circles had been played out. Some men routinely took advantage of the females under their roof, as Miss Lavender, in her role as directress of the Haven of Hope, would be the first to confirm.

If I was correct, and Mrs. Hargrove was Molly's mother, did she keep herself apprised of her daughter's life? If so, surely she would know of the girl's attachment to the lieutenant, know of their desire to marry. Living in the Jacombe house, she was also sure to have learned of the proposed duel. The gossip amongst servants spreads even more quickly than gossip in the *Beau Monde*.

Could the capable Mrs. Hargrove have taken matters into her own hands? Was she loyal to her daughter, or to her employer who might very well have been the girl's father?

❧ 15 ❧

Per my instructions, Ned and Ted set me down in Half Moon Street, necessitating a change in my thoughts.

A plump maid answered my knock on Mrs. Roucliffe's door. The servant was all smiles as she led me through the hall to a smallish sitting room overdone in shades of peach and coral.

Everything from the paint on the walls, the furniture, the carpet, and the bunches of roses in vases was done in varying shades of the same pinkish-orangey colour.

I bit back a laugh at Mrs. Roucliffe's idea of the setting for seduction. Then I chastised myself. Peach would be a flattering colour to the dark-haired Mrs. Roucliffe. Perhaps she was shrewd enough to know what colour surroundings would favour her looks.

A long peach-colored chaise dominated the area. Covered in slippery satin, it was undoubtedly intended for amorous pursuits. I could just imagine Foggie, the worse for drink, attempting to embrace his mistress and sliding off, falling flat on the floor.

The sounds of feminine voices caused me to look toward the hallway I had just come through. Mrs. Roucliffe stood with another woman. Perceiving my presence, she was about to motion her friend out the door. But that lady—I use the term loosely—had other ideas.

"Why, Cammie, you didn't tell me you had such a handsome visitor," she cooed to me. "I'm Angelica Nunn."

From the smell of gin coming from the puffy-featured blonde, I doubted there was anything angelic or nun-like about the woman. Past forty, and unable to deny it, she had resorted to the rouge-pot in a feeble attempt at a girlish glow. This served only to emphasise the lines spreading out like an open fan around her brown eyes. A more cruel person than I might say she was mutton dressed as lamb. The thought only crossed my mind, you see. I did not speak it.

"Good afternoon, Mrs. Nunn," I said in a cool tone while Mrs. Roucliffe looked on in amusement. "I am George Brummell."

"Very pleased to make your acquaintance," she replied with a slow smile of invitation.

Mrs. Roucliffe had had enough, though. "You were just leaving, Angelica. Come along. I want to have Mr. Brummell all to myself."

She ushered Mrs. Nunn out the door amidst much protest from that woman.

"I hope I was not interrupting anything," I said.

Mrs. Roucliffe indicated I should sit on the chaise. "Not at all. Poor Angelica was just complaining to me of her lover. She is looking for another *parti*. But let us not talk of her. You wanted to see me, no?" She sat next to me on the chaise and leaned close enough that I could smell her perfume. The scent was no more French than was the authenticity of her accent.

"Er, yes, I did," I said, feeling my intentions had been misunderstood. "I came to speak with you about Theobald Jacombe."

From the way Mrs. Roucliffe drew back, I could tell she thought her charms had brought me to her door and was disappointed they had not. "But why?"

"I am a curious sort of fellow, Mrs. Roucliffe. I find the arrest of Lieutenant Nevill too convenient. I should like to know more about the murder victim in order to find out who really killed him."

"Maybe his wife," Mrs. Roucliffe said, her face hardening. "God knows, she would have reason. But no, she is too innocent, he kept her too sheltered. She had no idea what he was really like."

"And you do?"

"I knew enough that I refused to accept a position as his mistress."

"Why did you do that, Mrs. Roucliffe?"

She suddenly became playful again. I did not envy Foggie this lover, a woman whose moods could be so mercurial. "La, there wasn't enough in it for me, *n'est-ce pas*? I do not mean money, for there was plenty of that. No, I engaged in a little dalliance with Jacombe, only to discover he was, how shall I say, *tres petit*."

Good God. "I believe I understand."

She laughed and leaned toward me with the air of a conspirator. "It might have done John, Count Boruwlaski, the dwarf, proud."

"So he offered to pay you a lot of money, did he?" I said, desperate to change the subject.

"Did you want a glass of wine? I see my maid neglected to bring you one."

"No, I am fine, thank you. Did Mr. Jacombe offer you a fine house?"

Again, she laughed. "Indeed, he did. In Richmond. Imagine, all the way out there. He wanted to keep me tucked away in a cage. A true Bird of Paradise."

"But you refused."

She nodded, a little more serious again. "You really are interested in what happened to him."

"Yes."

Her face changed then to a more serious expression, adding at least five years to her age. "There was a vein of cruelty in Theobald Jacombe. I have seen enough in my life to recognise it. Nothing, no amount of money, nor fancy house and servants, could induce me to the life he would have subjected me to."

"Do you know if he set up another paramour?"

"No one that I knew." She slanted a look at me. Flirting again. "Would you like to stay for a while, Mr. Brummell? We could have a little supper together. Later."

I rose. "You honour me, but I have a previous engagement."

"Another time?"

"Good afternoon, Mrs. Roucliffe," I said noncommittally, taking my leave.

I gave the order for home to Ned and Ted, wondering about Theobald Jacombe. His reputation in Society was spotless, yet he had been cheating at cards that night at my club, had been involved in a questionable banking transaction that had cost the Nevills a fortune, had possibly fathered a child by his housekeeper, and had been refused an offer of protection by a courtesan because of his cruelty. The deeper I dug into his life, the darker Jacombe's character became.

If only I could find the one person who had put an end to his existence.

I stayed at home just long enough to pick up a bundle of freshly laundered shirts to take to Lieutenant Nevill. Robinson tried to detain me.

"Sir, how long do you suppose Mrs. Ed will be with us?"

"How should I know? She only arrived three days ago."

"Three days?" he sighed dramatically. "I thought it was three months."

"Cut line and give over, man. Has she really given you any trouble?" I could have bitten off my tongue the moment the words were out of my mouth.

"She shot a rabbit in Hyde Park this morning, then sent André home early so she could prepare it herself for our dinner tonight. André was none too pleased about it, nor was he pleased about the lecture she read him on how food should be boiled, not sautéed. She told the laundress the starch in her boys' linen was too heavy and would give them neck aches. And she wanted to know why I would not cut the twins' hair, since I performed that service for you."

I edged toward the door. "I shall not be home for dinner. Tell André he is the best chef I have ever had in my employ, instruct the laundress not to change a single thing about the way she cleans our linen, and let the twins know their hair is handsome enough to be worn rather long. Oh, and do not wait up for me, I shall be late in returning."

I slipped outside before he could say another word. I

would have to avoid my own house for the remainder of the day.

I took a hackney coach to King's Bench Prison, where I found Molly alone with Lieutenant Nevill. I experienced a qualm at interrupting them. "I am sorry for intruding. I did not know you would be here, Molly."

"That's all right, Mr. Brummell. I'm sure Nicky is happy to see you."

"I am that. Thank you for the shirts. Did you visit my grandfather?"

I took a step farther into the small cell. "I have spoken with him twice. He is a crusty old fellow."

"I warned you," the lieutenant said.

I glanced casually at Molly. It would not do for her to know the motivation behind my next remarks. "You must be thankful not to be plagued by relatives, Molly."

The girl gave a half smile. "That's true. I never looked at it that way."

"So you do not know who either of your parents are?" I said, still in the most offhand way.

"No. The couple who took care of me said they were just ordinary, poor people. Apparently they weren't married and made a mistake. Me."

The lieutenant wrapped an arm around her waist. "It's no mistake as far as I'm concerned."

So the girl knew nothing. It was for the best, I judged.

I cleared my throat. "To return to the topic of your grandfather, Lieutenant Nevill, I have spoken to him on two occasions."

"And he won't help me," the soldier stated.

"Let us say he is being reticent at present."

"I told you he doesn't care about me."

I shook my head. "I would not say that at all. He helped your family through that situation with the banking deal that went bad."

The lieutenant's face reflected surprise. "How did you find out about that? I'd almost forgotten it."

"I told him, Nicky," Molly said.

"Yes, she did," I said. "We need any scrap of information that might help us find out who really killed Theobald Jacombe."

"But how could that old scandal have anything to do with what's happening now?" the lieutenant asked.

I paced for a moment, then looked the soldier in the eye. "Do you think there is any possibility that your grandfather is the one who killed Mr. Jacombe?"

"What!"

"Oh, Nicky!" Molly cried. "What if he did?"

"This is preposterous," the soldier declared.

"Now, listen to me. Your grandfather knows he does not have much longer to live. He harbours a grudge against Jacombe over the money he had to turn over to pay bank debts. Jacombe got away without paying anything, you know. Now he hears that the older, more experienced Jacombe is going to fight a duel with his grandson." I spread my hands in a gesture that invited the lieutenant to consider my words.

He looked at the floor for a moment. Then, slowly he said, "I suppose anything is possible. But why leave me here in the gaol? Why not turn himself in?"

"He's hateful, that's why," Molly said.

"I have thought of that," I said. "Mayhaps he wants to teach you a lesson. Could he just be putting his affairs in order?"

Lieutenant Nevill ran a hand through his hair. "His affairs are in order, as far as I know."

"Do you inherit everything?"

He shrugged. "Unless the old man's changed his will, yes."

"I wouldn't put it past him to have left everything to someone else. He hates the idea of Nicky marrying me," Molly said.

Lieutenant Nevill smiled at her. "You are the only thing I care about."

I cleared my throat. "Does your grandfather keep a lot of guns?"

"Several. He's always been worried about intruders since he likes to live alone."

"But you did not recognise the gun you found in the grass as one of his."

"No, but I've never looked at his pistols carefully."

"Very well. That is enough for today unless you can think of anything else."

"What will you do, Mr. Brummell?" the lieutenant asked.

"Find you a barrister. Keep investigating. Your grandfather is not the only person who did not like Mr. Jacombe. All I have to do is find the one person who disliked him enough to kill him."

16

Saturday afternoon I went to pay a call on Miss Lavender at the Haven of Hope. Lionel met me at the door. He looked worried.

"Good afternoon, Lion."

"Mr. Brummell, I'm glad to see you. I expect you've come to visit Miss Lavender, what with you bein' sweet on her and all."

"Ahem. I have told you before, I hold Miss Lavender in high esteem, but we are not, er, we are not—"

"Sure you ain't." He shot me a skeptical glance. "Anyways, she went shoppin'. I don't think she'll be back 'til evenin'.

"Deuce take it. I did want to see her. Oh, well, I suppose I can call on her tomorrow. What is wrong with you, Lion? You look blue-deviled."

The boy shuffled his feet. "Can you stay a few minutes and talk to me?"

"Certainly. Go ahead."

"It's private-like."

"Oh, of course."

I led him down to Miss Lavender's cluttered office, where two upholstered chairs angled toward the empty fireplace. Motioning for him to sit opposite me, I said, "Now what is this about?"

Once settled in his chair, Lionel paused a minute before finally speaking. "Somethin's still wrong with Miss Lavender. She's been behavin' mighty peculiar."

"What do you mean? She witnessed a dreadful scene the other night at Vauxhall. We talked about this before. Naturally she is upset," I said.

Even though I tried to reassure him, I knew myself that Miss Lavender had been very different since Mr. Jacombe's body had come over that waterfall.

Lionel rubbed his hand over the arm of the chair. "Tellin' things sure is 'ard."

I was immediately on alert. This was serious. The boy had something to confide, and he had chosen me to listen. I must show him respect and honour whatever he told me. Otherwise he would never trust me again. "I know it can be difficult to speak of private matters. I am honoured that you trust me enough to confide in me. I assure you, as a gentleman, that your trust is not misplaced."

The boy fixed me with a serious look. "I been watchin' 'er. I know it ain't nice, but I been that worried."

"You are too hard on yourself. If you have reason to be concerned, then keeping an eye on someone you care about can be a good thing."

"I can't say whether it's good or not." He leaned forward in his chair. "Miss Lavender has been goin' to Mr. Jacombe's grave at night."

"What?" Of all the words I thought might be ready to come from the boy's mouth, this idea never crossed my mind.

"For the past two nights, she's been doin' it."

"You had better tell me everything. Start at the beginning."

"You know Miss Lavender has a small bedchamber 'ere at the shelter."

"No, I did not know that. I know she stays here some nights, but I did not know she has her own room."

"Well, she does. A tiny room at the top in the attics. Anyhow, I went up there to talk to 'er the night before last, just before she was goin' 'ome. When I got to the room, the door was open. The room was lit by one candle. I didn't mean to spy or nothin'."

"I understand."

"I would 'ave let 'er know I was there, but she was kneelin' down in front of 'er bed. There was a steel box on the bed in front of 'er, a locked box. I know because she 'ad the key on a gold chain round 'er neck."

"So she was unlocking the box with the key around her neck?"

" 'Zactly. That's how I knew it was a private thing. I should 'ave left then, but I didn't."

"I expect you should have. But then we are only human. Curiosity got the better of you, is that it?"

"Uh-huh."

"But that is all right under the circumstances, you understand."

Lionel nodded.

"Go on, then."

"I was in the shadows where she couldn't see me. She

unlocked the box, and in the candlelight I could see what was in it."

I found I was holding my breath. Miss Lavender is such an open, frank girl. The whole idea of her having a secret she wished locked away was intriguing.

Lionel looked at me, his eyes rounded. "The box 'eld scraps of material. All of it looked the same, a bluish colour. I scratched my 'ead, expecting love letters or somethin', I suppose. But no, all that was in the box were these squares of cloth."

"Squares of cloth? What can this be about? What happened then?"

"Miss Lavender took one of the squares and put it in 'er pocket. Then she locked the box, put it under 'er bed, and put on a 'ooded cape. She was going to leave the shelter. I decided to follow 'er."

"And she went to Mr. Jacombe's grave?"

Lionel nodded. "And worse, you won't believe what she did, but I swears it's true."

"What did she do?"

"She got to the grave, took the square of material out of 'er pocket, and buried it in the fresh mound of dirt."

I drew back. "Lionel, are you absolutely certain of this?"

"I told you you wouldn't believe me!"

"Calm down now, I do believe you, I give you my word. It is just that I am surprised and cannot think of an explanation for Miss Lavender's actions."

"Me neither, that's why I'm tellin' you. 'Cause she went and did the very same thing last night."

"Good God!"

"It's true. I watched 'er upstairs, then followed 'er to the grave again. She's buryin' pieces of that material in Mr. Jacombe's grave, I tell you. And it don't make no sense to me."

"Nor to me. What time did this happen?"

"Both nights it were about eleven of the clock. What should we do?"

"I shall follow her tonight and see what I can discover. Let me handle it."

"I want to come with you."

"No, Lionel. There are some things I should do on my own. This is one of them."

"Miss Lavender will be all right, won't she?" Lionel asked, his face reflecting his concern.

"We shall make sure that she is."

I made the rounds of White's—avoiding Fairingdale's insinuating remarks—and Watier's that evening, but I was really just biding my time until I could follow Miss Lavender.

At Watier's, I found Lords Petersham and Munro. They had finished dinner and were enjoying white port and brandied cherries.

Petersham eyed me with sympathy. "Looks like your young friend is up to his ears in trouble."

"His neck is what will be experiencing the most difficulty, I expect," Munro quipped. "When they put the rope around it."

"Is there some new information?" I asked, picking up a cherry and popping it into my mouth.

Petersham took a sip of port, then said, "You know, Brummell, all of London is crying for Nevill's head. I shouldn't be surprised at a speedy trial at King's Bench."

"And the Lord Chief Justice is not one to tarry when it comes to handing down a sentence. Especially when we are speaking of such a heinous crime," Munro said.

He was right, deuce take it. Unless I could soon find out who really pulled the trigger and killed Mr. Jacombe, I could find myself up against a trial and an even faster execution of Lieutenant Nevill.

I contented myself with telling them a lot could happen between now and then, before changing the topic to that of the food at the club.

Afterward, I conversed with several other members of Watier's, discovering opinion was universal that the young soldier would find himself at the end of a rope before a week had passed. There were pages of wagers in the Betting Book over at White's on it.

Putting these glum predictions aside for a while, at half-past ten I positioned myself across New Street from where the Haven of Hope is located. I remained in the shadows so that Miss Lavender would not perceive I was following her. The streets, lit only by oil lamps, were dark, but my gleaming white cravat might stand out in the darkness and give me away were I to get too close to her.

At precisely eleven of the clock, Miss Lavender emerged from the shelter. Clad in a lightweight, dark-coloured hooded cloak, exactly like Lionel had reported, she made her way through the streets in a westerly direction with me behind her.

Due north of Hyde Park, we reached the St. George's Burial Ground at the back of St. George's Row. I had attended the burial of Mr. Jacombe, so I knew where his grave was located. Therefore, I was able to stay back and allow her to enter the graveyard well ahead of me. Then I followed. I walked slowly and with care as to where my steps took me. I did not want the crunch of my boots to give me away.

Many of the headstones were large enough to conceal me. Thus, when I was in sight of Miss Lavender, I simply positioned my body behind one of them, giving a silent apology to the deceased beneath me.

Again, exactly as Lionel had described, Miss Lavender removed a scrap of cloth from the folds of her dress. In the eerie light of the cemetery, she knelt beside the grave, and using her bare hands, she moved some of the dirt aside, placed the material in the hollow, then covered it with earth.

She stood and paused for a moment, gazing down at the grave. My imagination might have been at work, but I swear I thought I could see her green gaze staring with uncharacteristic loathing at Mr. Jacombe's headstone.

Then, with a swirling of cape, she turned and retraced her steps out of the burial ground.

I remained where I was, torn between confronting her and some deep feeling of dread.

What was this all about?

Did I really want to know?

Of course, I chastised myself, I must know, for it might have bearing on the investigation. Yet I had to admit that my feelings for Miss Lavender went beyond the casual. I found that I did not want to uncover something that might alter those feelings.

Still, I would at least follow her home to be certain that she was safe.

With that object in mind, I hurried out of the graveyard and down the street, only to see her climbing into a hackney-coach.

I felt sure she would go home to Fetter Lane now, and that was too great a distance to walk.

I watched the coach move off in an easterly direction until I could no longer hear the noise of the horses' hooves on the stone road.

I walked back to Mr. Jacombe's grave, stripped off my gloves, and parted the earth with my fingers. I found one of the scraps of material without much effort.

Folding the fabric neatly in half, I wrapped it inside my handkerchief and placed it in my pocket before heading off on some private pursuits.

No, I do not wish to tell you about them. Recall that I wanted to avoid my own home for the rest of the evening. That is all I care to divulge. A gentleman's code of honour, you understand.

As for what Miss Lavender's secret was, I would not uncover it this night.

❧ 17 ❧

Sunday morning after church services were over, I took myself to the Jacombe house. I had little interest in seeing the widow or her trusted physician at the present moment. Instead, I wished to question the housekeeper, Mrs. Hargrove, to see if my suspicions where she was concerned were correct.

The butler admitted me and showed me once again to the green-and-ivory sitting-room. Mrs. Hargrove's face reflected no surprise at being asked to attend me.

"You must be wondering why I asked to see you, Mrs. Hargrove," I said.

"How can I serve you, sir?" she asked. Ever efficient.

"I have a delicate matter to discuss with you. Will you sit down, please?"

The housekeeper sat at the edge of a chair facing the sofa. The idea that it might well be a rare occasion for her to sit in this room took hold in my head. I sat down opposite her and studied the tidy woman for a moment. There was no anxiety in her expression at this unusual circumstance. I marveled at her self-control. I judged her to be the type not likely to be tricked into admitting anything she wanted to conceal. Thus, I came directly to the point.

"Mrs. Hargrove, Mrs. Jacombe told me that you were with child during the first year of your employment in this household."

A tiny flicker of surprise, quickly extinguished, was the only show of emotion on the housekeeper's face. "I was."

"Molly has your eyes."

There was no reaction to the name of her daughter. I realised I had made a statement, one Mrs. Hargrove obviously felt she need not respond to. I tried again. "Molly, the girl betrothed to Lieutenant Nevill, is your daughter, is she not?"

Mrs. Hargrove's face remained a mask.

"May I remind you, there is a murder investigation going on, Mrs. Hargrove? Bow Street might find even the most remote piece of information, such as the names of Molly's parents, of interest. I propose that we keep the information between ourselves for the moment."

"I am of the understanding that Bow Street has Mr. Jacombe's killer in custody," she said.

"And I am of the opinion that they do not," I told her. "Now, if we can return to the topic of Molly's parentage."

"I gave birth to her, yes," she relented.

The words were spoken calmly, but I could feel a tension growing in the housekeeper. "I see you do not want that fact made public. I shall try to oblige you in the matter."

"You will have to since you have no proof."

"Are you saying that you would deny the fact in court?"

"If need be to protect Mrs. Jacombe. I owe her that."

"Ah, I see. So I am correct in assuming that Mr. Jacombe was Molly's father."

"Of course. I have never had another lover."

I looked at the cold, emotionless woman in front of me. "He kept you here."

"He kept me here because I threatened to tell his new bride that he was the father of my child. I was desperate. Pregnant servants face living in the streets."

"I know," I said, forcing myself to adopt the same tone and economy of words as the housekeeper. "He paid for a couple to raise Molly."

"That was part of our arrangement."

"Did you remain lovers?"

"Certainly not. Once I determined what sort of man he was, I ended the affair immediately."

"Why did you remain in his employ?"

"He paid me well."

"And you kept this secret all these years. Did you keep up with your daughter's life?"

"Not really. I knew she was being cared for, and that was all that mattered. I had to cut off any sentimental feelings where she was concerned."

I wondered then if a mother ever could dissolve all feelings for a daughter. "But then Mr. Jacombe must have stopped paying for the girl's upkeep."

Mrs. Hargrove's mouth tightened. "He used to watch her from a distance. Not out of any fatherly concern, but because he always had a lust for young female flesh. Once he saw she had grown beautiful, he stopped the payments. He said she could fend for herself."

"That was about a year or so ago, was it not?"

"Yes. There was nothing I could do about it even had I wanted to. Which I did not."

"I have a slight acquaintance with the girl. She now lives at a shelter for women, the Haven of Hope. Employers have found her too attractive in the past, and she makes herself useful while continuing her education at the shelter."

This information was met with no apparent interest whatsoever.

"Mrs. Hargrove, were you not angry at Mr. Jacombe for what he did to you?"

"He seduced me, and I fell victim to his words of love. That was my mistake."

"What of his treatment of Molly? Had he not stopped the payments to the couple raising her, she would still have a home."

"She is alive and is in good health."

"But her betrothed may very well end up on the gallows. Do you not care?"

"I cannot afford to care, as I have already intimated to you, Mr. Brummell. If that is all, I have to confer with Cook regarding the evening meal."

"I have nothing else to ask at this time. I shall keep this conversation between us, since it is obvious you do not want Molly to know you are her mother."

"Thank you." Mrs. Hargrove rose and exited the room quietly.

I sat motionless. My immediate thoughts were not of Mrs. Hargrove, but of my own father. She reminded me of him in many ways. He had been cold and unemotional as well. Except for when he was taking me to task for some misdemeanour. Then he could be quite fierce in his opinions.

What, I wondered, could cause a parent to behave thus?

Perhaps in the case of Mrs. Hargrove, she had no choice but to sever all ties to her baby. She could not afford to do otherwise, as she had said.

Regarding my own father, I suspected he would forever remain an enigma to me. I would do better to focus on the investigation.

I could easily think of two motives that would drive Mrs. Hargrove to shoot Mr. Jacombe at Vauxhall Pleasure Gardens. First, if she heard about the impending duel—and there was no doubt in my mind the news had travelled through all classes of Londoners quicker than thought—then she would not want her daughter's betrothed wounded or possibly killed by the girl's father. That, in and of itself, would have been motivation to stop Mr. Jacombe.

Secondly, though she denied any sort of bitterness toward Mr. Jacombe, accepting responsibility for her own actions, surely she had not forgiven him for getting her with child.

Then there was the fact that Mr. Jacombe had ceased paying for the girl's upbringing when Molly had reached sixteen. Though she denied any feeling, Mrs. Hargrove must have had some lingering sense of anger about that. While too many years might have gone by for her to go to Mrs. Jacombe with her sordid story now, perhaps she saw another way to get her revenge.

It would have been simple enough for the efficient housekeeper to slip away to Vauxhall Pleasure Gardens and put a period to Mr. Jacombe's life. That way he could not hurt Molly or any other female again.

This last observation caused my thoughts to abruptly veer in another direction.

Mrs. Hargrove said that Mr. Jacombe had always lusted after young females.

Suddenly Miss Lavender's expression of shock at Mr. Jacombe's death, her interest in the investigation, the scene last night at Mr. Jacombe's grave, all flashed through my mind in rapid succession.

Miss Lavender and Mr. Jacombe.

Oh no.

❧ 18 ❧

I went to the Haven of Hope first, though I had little reason to think Miss Lavender would be there on a Sunday afternoon. She normally spent the Sabbath with her father in their snug rooms in Fetter Lane.

Perhaps it was the desire not to exchange volleys with Mr. Lavender that caused me to stop by the shelter on the chance Miss Lavender might be there. As I had surmised, though, she was not. Miss Ashton was in charge.

I directed the hackney-coach to take me to Fetter Lane. I had left Ned and Ted and my sedan-chair at home. My plan was to take Miss Lavender to Hyde Park, where I might find a quiet place to talk with her privately.

The sun shone and the day was warm. I let down the glass of the coach so that a breeze might come through and freshen the air. I heard the cries of street vendors and directed the coachman to stop the vehicle.

I alighted and purchased a small bunch of violets for Miss Lavender. Once the coach lumbered along again, I looked down at the flowers in my hand and thought of Miss Lavender with her porcelain-like skin and fascinating green eyes.

Part of me did not want to hear what had happened between her and Mr. Jacombe, but the wheels of the coach rolled on, taking me closer to Fetter Lane.

When we stopped in front of Kint's Chop House, I paid the coachman to wait for me. Around back, a set of steps led to the Lavenders' rooms. I climbed them, holding the flowers.

At my knock, Mr. Lavender came to the door. He was in his shirtsleeves and his usual corduroy pants tucked into scratched boots. A crumb of what I thought was oatcake rested in his mustache. He held one of his collection of pipes in his hand.

"Good afternoon," I said cheerfully. "Lovely day, is it not? I thought at once of your daughter. I have come to take Miss Lavender to Hyde Park, if she would care for it."

Mr. Lavender scowled. "What did I tell you just the other day outside Gunter's?"

I tilted my head as if to consider the matter. "That you have the wrong man in gaol for the murder of Mr. Jacombe?"

He used the pipe to gesture at me. "I have the right man in gaol and the wrong man on my doorstep."

"Well, naturally, I did not kill Mr. Jacombe," I said, taking an unholy glee in confounding the Bow Street man.

"Would that I could pin that on you, more's the pity. But sure as the sun is shining, Lieutenant Nevill will face the Lord Chief Justice. There's no doubt in my mind what will happen next."

"An innocent man will be convicted for a crime while the murderer goes free?"

Mr. Lavender's brows came together. "A guilty man, the one we have in custody, will be hanged, but you run around amusing yourself trying to prove me wrong in the meantime. Just leave my daughter out of it."

"Father, is that Mr. Brummell at the door?" Miss Lavender's voice called. She appeared in the doorway behind her frowning father. She is nearsighted and squinted at me. I wondered why she did not have on the spectacle-glasses I had had made for her. Perhaps she did not have to use them all the time.

Clad in a simple pale blue gown, her dark red hair pinned loosely at the crown of her head, she made me draw in my breath at her beauty.

"Miss Lavender, forgive me for calling without prior agreement, but the day is so fine, I thought you might enjoy a walk in Hyde Park. These are for you, by the way," I said, handing her the violets around her father's beefy shoulder.

I could almost see thoughts in his head of snatching the flowers away from her and slamming the door in my face. I smiled at him strictly to annoy him.

"Why, these are pretty, Mr. Brummell. Thank you. I'll put them in water and get my shawl."

"Oh, you will not need to cover up, Miss Lavender. The day is quite warm, I assure you," I called after her.

"Take the shawl if you must go, Lydia," her father instructed. He did not invite me inside.

Miss Lavender was back in a moment, sans shawl. She kissed her father on his outraged cheek. "I'll be home in time to fix your supper, Father."

"Take care, Lydia," Mr. Lavender advised, glaring at me.

Much to my surprise, we made it into the coach without Mr. Lavender charging after us. Miss Lavender sat on the seat opposite me. As soon as we were under way, she turned the force of her green gaze on me. "I assume you wished to speak to me about Lieutenant Nevill."

"In part. I confess I simply want to be with you."

"You didn't last Thursday at Gunter's. You left me so you could speak with that brunette."

"That had to do with the investigation."

"Faith, you don't expect me to believe that, do you?"

"Yes, I do. I expect you to believe what I tell you because I am truthful with you."

She bit her lip and said nothing.

We travelled in silence to the gates of Hyde Park. I paid the driver, adding a generous tip.

The fashionable hour to be seen in Hyde Park is generally around five in the afternoon in the spring and summer. Though it was only three, the Park was still full of people of all classes. Children rolled hoops, ladies walked in the company of gentlemen, couples rode slowly in open carriages, and all around us the Park was green, dotted with the colours of various flowers.

I took Miss Lavender's arm and slipped it through mine, enjoying the feel of her small hand on me. Past the Serpentine River we walked while I chatted to her about the dress or behaviour of various people we saw.

At last I spied a bench nearly hidden by the leaves of a great oak tree.

"Come, let us sit down in the shade," I said.

She took her hand from my arm. Instantly I missed it.

We sat down on the bench, her skirts touching my leather breeches.

"Do you have news regarding Jacombe's death?" she asked.

"I have someone whom I think had the motive to kill him."

She leaned toward me. "Who?"

"Mrs. Hargrove, the housekeeper at the Jacombe house," I said, looking into her eyes. I did not want to break contact with her gaze. I wanted to see her reaction, to let her know that, while I did not necessarily want to know her secret, that I did indeed know, and I would be strong for her.

"Why would this Mrs. Hargrove want to kill her employer?" she asked, but I could see the answer growing in the back of her mind.

"It could have been one of several reasons. You see, and I say this to you in confidence, Mr. Jacombe got Mrs. Hargrove with child soon after she came into his employ some eighteen years ago."

Miss Lavender looked away. "I see."

"She is Molly's mother."

Miss Lavender jumped up from the bench.

I rose immediately.

"Molly's mother?" she said, her hand going to her throat. "Molly's mother—and then that means that—that—Jacombe is Molly's father!"

"Yes, though Molly need not ever know." I reached out and took her hand, which I noticed was trembling. I held it in a firm, but reassuring grip. "Mrs. Hargrove might have murdered Mr. Jacombe, trying to protect Molly's betrothed. Or it could have been revenge. The need for revenge could have eaten away at her and culminated when Jacombe stopped paying the people who were caring for Molly when she was sixteen, leaving her to the streets."

Miss Lavender looked at me then. "He did not throw Mrs.

Hargrove out of the house when she was with child. Did they remain lovers?"

"No. She threatened to expose him to his wife if he made her leave."

"Oh, he would not have wanted so much as a hint of impropriety to touch his name," Miss Lavender said with bitterness. "Always the principled man, the honourable man, was Mr. Jacombe."

"Mrs. Hargrove loathed him. She said that he lusted for young females. I imagine he took advantage of them whenever he could."

Miss Lavender's face, more translucent than my finest Sèvres porcelain, went entirely white.

❦ 19 ❦

Still holding her hand, I eased her back down to the bench, fearing she might faint. I had to get her to tell me what had transpired between them, even though I felt I already knew. I could not help but believe she needed to share the burden with someone for her own sake, if nothing else, just as I was certain she had never done so before.

Her gaze was turned away from me. I knew she was remembering whatever had happened, and I hated Mr. Jacombe. "Tell me, Miss Lavender."

She turned to me. "Tell you what?"

"Have I not earned your trust in the years we have known one another? Have I ever given you cause to doubt my loyalty to you as my friend?"

"No," she said, tears forming in her eyes. "You are different than any man I've ever known other than Father."

"I shall take that as a compliment. Now listen to me. Out of concern, I followed you last night. I saw you go to Jacombe's grave." I pulled yesterday's handkerchief out and unwrapped the scrap of blue material within.

Her tears flowed freely at the sight of it, down her porcelain cheeks to splash on her dress.

I reached for my fresh handkerchief, but knew she needed to cry. I sat quietly with one arm lightly around her shoulder while she wept.

When she stopped, I used the handkerchief to dry her cheeks as if she were a small child. She accepted this treatment, then seemed to gather her strength.

"I was fifteen years old. Father was struggling to further his career in Bow Street. I knew Mr. Jacombe was an important man and could help Father. They would meet at our rooms and talk about the crime in London and what could be done about it. I would serve tea or coffee and cakes. My mother had died the previous year, you see."

"So you acted as hostess for your father."

"Yes. Mr. Jacombe was always polite to me, as I was to him. He was in his middle thirties, not as stout then, and had a kind way of looking at me. He seemed interested in my thoughts and would often ask me my opinion of one thing or another while I was pouring tea. I felt important around him, and I felt that I was helping Father."

"It must have been a heady combination of feelings for a young girl who had just lost her mother."

She nodded. "One day he came to our rooms when Father was out. He seemed content to talk with me for, oh, I don't know, perhaps a quarter of an hour, asking me about my interests, talking to me about what an intelligent man my father was. I was flattered to think this important man would care to converse with me."

"It would only be natural for you to feel that way."

"Do you think so?" she asked me.

"Of course. A young girl whose mother has gone out of her life and who is now taking care of her father. Of course she would be charmed by a man of distinction showing an interest in her. Come, Miss Lavender, you have surely heard of many such cases in your work at the shelter."

"I have. I suppose I just never thought of myself in that way. As vulnerable."

"Are you not as human as everyone else?"

"I should have known what he was about, and I didn't!" she exclaimed.

"No, you were an innocent and could not have known."

She spoke faster now. "He started coming to our rooms more often when Father was not there. He would take tea with me, talk with me. I—I started to have warm feelings toward him, to look forward to his visits."

"Which he asked you to keep secret from your father."

"Yes! This was our private time, something special just between the two of us, he would assure me. Then one day, I remember the date, the sixteenth of May, he came to me. We were laughing over something silly when he slowly leaned over and kissed me on the lips. I didn't pull away, much to my eternal shame."

"You were curious, as all girls are at that age. And this was a man in your family's trust."

"Oh, yes, I trusted him. What a fool I was. A little fool! For once he started kissing me, he did not stop. Even when I grew frightened and asked him to stop, begged him to stop. His hands were suddenly everywhere, he had me on the sofa and was on top of me before I could think what was happening. It was over quickly, then he threatened me. He said that if I ever told my father, he would make sure that Father was dismissed from Bow Street."

She looked at me then. "I have never told another living soul any of this. I don't know why I've told you."

"Were not Theobald Jacombe already dead, I would kill him for you, Miss Lavender," I said.

I meant my words. Something inside me seemed to break open and release itself into my veins when Miss Lavender told me her story. I wanted to protect her, to understand her, and to give comfort to her. I feared I did not know how to do this, that I would fall short of what she needed from me right now.

"He is dead, so you need not trouble yourself over something that happened seven years ago, Mr. Brummell."

"Understand this, Miss Lavender. There was nothing you could have done to prevent what happened. You were this man's victim. I have no doubt he planned a seduction from the moment he laid eyes on you. You are not to blame in any way for his evil."

"Everyone thinks him such a great man!"

"Evil takes many forms, you know that now. One cannot often easily recognise it. That does not make one a fool."

"Perhaps you're right," she said doubtfully.

"I know I am. And look what a brave girl you are. This is why you started your shelter, is it not? To help other girls who had been victims at the hands of evil men."

"Yes. Yes, that is why! I don't want them to feel the loneliness, the isolation, the shame I felt after it happened."

I still held the blue material in my hand. "Tell me about this."

"The gown I had on that day was bloodied after Mr. Jacombe was done with me. I had to get rid of it so Father wouldn't see, yet I could not bring myself to put it in the dustbin. I needed it somehow, I can't explain my feelings.

I cut it into pieces, throwing the majority of it away, but keeping part of it in a locked box. After his death, I was seized with the desire to bury what was left of the gown with him. I don't have the answers as to why I am doing it. Mayhaps keeping the gown was a reminder to always be on my guard, to never let another man close to me. Now I want to let the past stay in the past."

"You have never had a, er, warm relationship with any other man then?"

"No. I never believed I could trust a man. Until now," she said, looking at me.

I cannot tell you the deep sense of pride and honour I felt when she spoke those last two words. She had given me one of the most precious of treasures, one I would have to guard closely.

"You honour me, Miss Lavender. I shall not betray you."

"I'm not a young girl anymore, Mr. Brummell. You need not treat me as though I will break."

At these words, she leaned toward me. I was gripped with a desire to kiss her, yet something held me back. I did not want to hurt her in any way. What would it mean to her if I kissed her? More than she wanted? More than I could give?

But the independent Miss Lavender settled the matter for me. One small hand slipped around my neck and pulled me to her. At the taste of her lips, the feel of her soft mouth, I pushed aside any doubts and kissed her. Pleasure radiated outward from our joined mouths, sending waves of desire through me.

I pulled away.

Miss Lavender put a finger across my lips. "I want nothing from you. Remember, I am no longer a young girl."

But she was still innocent in some ways for all of her two-

and-twenty years, I thought. "I hold you in high esteem, Miss Lavender."

Her expression brightened a bit. "Good. Then you won't have the slightest objection to our finding Mr. Jacombe's killer and freeing the lieutenant together. Together, Mr. Brummell. You can see now why I have such a fevered interest in this case."

"Well, I—"

"I thought you wouldn't object. I'll question Father this evening and see what he knows about the lieutenant's trial. I'm not certain, but I think with the hue and cry all over London, the Lord Chief Justice will not wait long before hearing the matter."

No, he would not. Nor was there any reason to think that unless I could find out who really killed Mr. Jacombe, Lieutenant Nevill would be sentenced to death.

⁂ 20 ⁂

I hardly slept that night. I could not help but think of Mr. Jacombe's evil in connection with Miss Lavender. I found myself having mad thoughts of going to the burial ground, digging up his corpse, and wringing his neck.

It was a good thing that the horror Mr. Jacombe had inflicted on Miss Lavender was a secret, else she might be considered a suspect in his murder. The dastard.

What a different man Mr. Jacombe was turning out to be from the image he presented in Society. He had impregnated a servant in his employ, ravished a young girl—who knew how many others there were?—had been involved in that bad banking deal, cut off funds for the care of his natural child, had tried to set up a courtesan in an expensive house, was a partner in a bear-baiting ring, and had cheated at cards. The list seemed to go on endlessly.

Sleep did not come to me until the small hours of the morning; thus the hour had already advanced to the afternoon when I awoke. Chakkri presented himself to me for his morning petting and complimenting session. This is where I am forced to stroke his fawn-coloured body until he deems he has had enough. All the while I must tell him what a handsome animal he is, graceful, intelligent, and generally wonderful to have around.

Robinson walked into my chamber while this was going on. His lips pursed as they always do in connection with the cat. "Sir, I regret having to tell you this, but apparently we have an emergency situation on our hands."

"Oh, devil. Before I have even had my tea, Robinson?"

"I shall bring it to you presently, but I thought you should know that Winifred has a rash."

"Winifred? Who is Winifred?"

"Mrs. Ed's piglet."

"Good God, Robinson, what am I supposed to do about it?"

Chakkri butted his head against my hand. The one which had mistakenly ceased scratching behind his left ear.

"Mrs. Ed has been stomping about the kitchens, raising her voice at André. She says he should have some Smith's Swine Salve on hand. Sadly, he does not."

"I assume Smith's Swine Salve would cure what ails the pig?"

"Evidently, it is the only *oinkment* that will serve."

"Very funny. And why does Mrs. Ed not simply go out and purchase some of this salve in the market?"

"She claims it is only available back home in Dorset county."

I sighed. "Tell her I shall see what I can do."

"Yes, sir."

"Bring my tea now, Robinson. Oh, and hand me the cat's brush from the dressing-table before you go."

Robinson picked up the brush between two fingers and conveyed it to me, arm outstretched. He then left the room to avoid witnessing what was to follow.

Indeed, while the cat adores being brushed, he makes quite a game of it, walking away and then coming back and begging for more.

Clad in a paisley dressing gown, I spent the next quarter of an hour engaged in this pastime, while my mind was on the subject of Mr. Jacombe. Specifically, who had shot him at Vauxhall Pleasure Gardens.

All during The Dressing Hour, I remained preoccupied, murmuring a request for my Alexandria-blue coat and scolding Robinson for accepting a less than pristine shirt from the laundress, but really thinking only of who was most likely to have killed Mr. Jacombe.

Chakkri was curled on the bed with one brown velvet paw firmly over his eyes.

After dressing, I went downstairs to my bookroom to peruse my letters, when I came upon one from the very person who had most occupied my thoughts: Mr. Jacombe's killer. Inconsiderate person he or she was, no signature was on the letter, simply the following lines: *The Lieutenant's time is running out. Find a way to free him. I cannot come forward.*

The words were printed on fine paper, just as they had been in the first letter. I slapped it down on my desk in frustration. So the killer could not "come forward," eh? I expect not, when he or she knew a hangman's noose would be waiting.

A pounding on the front door distracted me. I folded the letter and put it in my desk drawer along with the other. I heard voices in the hall and glanced at my tall case clock. The hands indicated it was half-past two.

Robinson came into the room looking flustered. "Sir, Miss Lavender is here. Do you wish to see her?" he asked in a pinched voice. He cannot abide Miss Lavender's tendency to disregard the conventions. Unmarried females do not call at a bachelor's residence, you know.

"Of course I want to see her. Show her in immediately."

But Robinson did not need to trouble himself, for Miss Lavender had followed him into the room. She looked particularly fetching today in a moss-green gown cut with a square neck. The dress was more feminine than her usual more serviceable gowns. "Mr. Brummell, I came as soon as I could. I have news."

I rose. "Robinson, you may go now, unless Miss Lavender would like some tea." I raised a questioning brow.

"No, nothing, thank you," she said.

Robinson was forced to leave at this point, much to his sorrow, I was sure. Just as I was sure he would listen outside the door.

"Sit down, Miss Lavender, and tell me what has happened."

"There is no time. The lieutenant's grandfather went to Mr. Read early this morning."

"Mr. Nevill at Bow Street? Did he bail his grandson out of gaol?"

"No! He told Mr. Read that he'd seen *Molly* with a pistol that night at Vauxhall. He says he believes that Molly is the one who killed Mr. Jacombe, and that his grandson is merely taking the blame for his betrothed."

"The devil you say!"

"It's true."

"I would never have believed the old man would be so

crafty. Here he can release his grandson from gaol and rid himself of an unwanted future marriage."

"That's exactly what I think he's doing, and that's what I told Father when he came to my shelter for lunch."

"Is that how you found out about this, through your father?"

"Yes, but you've not heard the worst. When Mr. Read and Father told Lieutenant Nevill what his grandfather said, the lieutenant made a full confession! He claims he *did* kill Mr. Jacombe."

"Good God. The news will be all over London before Chakkri can turn a whisker."

"Molly was beside herself when she learned of this. I left her in the care of my assistant and came directly to you."

"I am glad you did. Let us go at once to King's Bench Prison and try to talk sense into the lieutenant."

But there was no reasoning with the soldier. He sat resolutely on the cot in his cell, refusing to even consider retracting his confession. "For they will put Molly in gaol, and that I can't have," was all he would say to my entreaties.

I questioned how Bow Street could believe the word of an old man who was partially blind. I begged Lieutenant Nevill to defend himself.

In vain, Miss Lavender and I spent the better part of three hours trying to talk sense to the young man, but he would not budge. He said it all did not matter anyway, since the barrister I had hired said there was nothing he could do unless we could nail down who did commit the murder.

"Then I will go to your grandfather myself and make him retract his statement," I finally said. "Come, Miss Lavender."

The hour was after six when we left King's Bench Prison

and made our way through the crowded streets to Mr. Nevill's rooms.

I used my dog's head walking stick to knock on the door, but there was no reply.

"Mr. Nevill is a known recluse," I explained to Miss Lavender. "I cannot believe he is out and about at this hour."

"Perhaps he is sleeping. After all, he's had a busy day, pointing the finger of guilt at an innocent girl."

"Mr. Nevill!" I said, raising my voice and knocking again. There was still no reply.

"Should we wait for him to return?" Miss Lavender asked.

I considered the question, a creeping sense of unease coming over me. "No. I have a feeling something is not right here. Mr. Nevill is old. The strain of today might have been too much for him. I, er, think you might want to turn your back."

"Turn my back? Whatever for?"

"So that you cannot see me committing the crime of entering a man's rooms without his permission."

"Oh," she said and turned around. "Do hurry."

I am not an expert at picking locks, though I have had occasion to do so a time or two since turning my hand to criminal investigations. I regret to say that at least five minutes passed before the portal swung open under my touch.

I walked across the threshold and immediately swung back around. "Do not come in here, Miss Lavender."

The intrepid Miss Lavender walked past me and gasped.

For there, in the centre of the sitting-room floor, was the dead body of Mr. Nevill.

He had been shot through the heart.

21

"*Lydia! What are* you doing here? And with Mr. Brummell, to make matters worse." These were Mr. Lavender's first words when he arrived upon the scene.

I had paid a boy on the street to find a constable, who, in turn, notified Mr. Lavender of this latest murder.

Miss Lavender kept a level head despite the circumstances. I could only admire her strength. She said, "We had to come here after what you told me about Mr. Nevill's accusations regarding Molly."

"Did you see who did this?" he asked.

"No," I said. "When we arrived, no one was about. The door was shut and locked."

"Really, now? How did you get in then?" Mr. Lavender asked, dreaming, perhaps, of hauling me before the Bow Street magistrate on charges of breaking and entering.

"Er, the door gave way with a bit of pressure," I dissembled. "Considering Mr. Nevill's advanced age, we were concerned when he did not answer our knock. I merely fiddled with the door a bit."

"Shot with his own gun, it looks like," Mr. Lavender said. "You saw no one?"

"No, Father. Who could have done this? Might it be the same person who killed Mr. Jacombe? That way, you must see that Lieutenant Nevill is not responsible. He cannot have killed Mr. Nevill when he is sitting in King's Bench Prison. And Mr. Nevill has been shot through the heart in exactly the same method the murderer used to kill Mr. Jacombe."

Mr. Lavender eyed his daughter sternly. "Now, Lydia, I don't want to argue with you, but it's very obvious who did this."

Miss Lavender's green eyes rounded. "Who?"

I suddenly knew exactly where Mr. Lavender's thoughts were headed. And I was right.

"Molly," Mr. Lavender said.

Miss Lavender was immediately outraged. "Father, you can't believe that! Besides, she's been at the shelter all day lying down."

"Molly is the one who had motive to kill both Mr. Jacombe and Mr. Nevill, actually," Mr. Lavender mused.

"Father! You are never saying you believe Molly guilty of committing a double murder!" Miss Lavender cried. "She's not capable of such a thing, I tell you."

Mr. Lavender looked at his daughter. "It could be that she is. She might have killed Mr. Jacombe because he was going to fight the lieutenant in that duel and because he had insulted her. She'd want Mr. Nevill dead because he had witnessed her with a gun in her possession. And, now that I come to think of it, because with Mr. Nevill out of the

way, I'm sure an inheritance will come into the young soldier's hand. She might have come here to try to reason with
the old man, then when she found she couldn't, she picked
up a gun and shot him."

"That is all well and good," I said. "But before we con-
demn a seventeen-year-old girl for all this plotting and murdering, let us go to the Haven of Hope and see if Molly is
resting in her bed, shall we?"

"Aye, that is what we'll do, all right," Mr. Lavender said.

"Yes, we will. And you will see, Father, that Molly has
been at the shelter all day long and could not have shot
anyone," Miss Lavender said.

We rode together in a hackney-coach, the tension thicker
than any fog.

"You know, Mr. Lavender, there are other suspects in the
case of who killed Mr. Jacombe," I said, while we rumbled
along toward New Street.

"Like who, laddie?"

"What about his wife?"

"That's possible," Miss Lavender said, looking at me
thoughtfully.

"No, it is not possible," Mr. Lavender replied stubbornly.
"She loved the man."

"That may be true. But I have discovered some unsavoury
activities that Mr. Jacombe was involved in." I reached over
in the dim light of the coach and touched Miss Lavender's
hand. I wanted to convey to her that I would not betray her
secret, and I wanted to offer her comfort. Fortunately for the
safety of my person, Mr. Lavender did not see the action.

"Like what?" Mr. Lavender asked.

I suddenly realised that if I told Mr. Lavender that Mrs.
Hargrove had a child by Mr. Jacombe and that child was

Molly, I would just give him yet another motive for the girl to have murdered him. Instead, I said, "He tried to set up an expensive mistress, a Mrs. Roucliffe."

Mr. Lavender glared at me as if I had bats in my attic. "Isn't that common practice? Wives look the other way, if they even know. From what I've gathered about Mrs. Jacombe, she is a naive, innocent sort who wouldn't even dream her husband would do wrong. No, laddie, it won't do. Besides, Mrs. Jacombe was at home the night her husband was shot."

"How do you know that?" I asked.

"Because she told me," he admitted.

"Did you ask for people to back up her story?"

"No, because we already have the killer," the Bow Street man said, his voice rising an octave.

"Which one?" I replied smoothly.

It was fortunate that at this juncture we arrived at the Haven of Hope. Alighting from the coach, I offered Miss Lavender my hand to assist her down, under her father's scowling gaze.

We entered the building and at once perceived Lionel and Miss Ashton, Miss Lavender's assistant, seated in the front sitting-room, which served as a classroom. Miss Ashton, a pretty blond-haired girl, was working with Lionel on his reading. Some of the other girls sat about sewing. Molly was nowhere in sight.

Miss Ashton rose at our entrance and came into the hall.

Mr. Lavender took command. "Miss Ashton, I must ask you a question. Has Molly been at the shelter all day today?"

Miss Ashton looked to each of us, a confused expression on her face. "Why, I expect so."

"You expect so?" Mr. Lavender said. "I'm afraid I need a

more definite answer. Either you know for a certainty that she was here, or you don't."

Growing more uncomfortable by the minute, Miss Ashton's words came out in a rush. "She went to bed earlier in the day, she was so upset over that old Mr. Nevill's nasty actions. I've been busy teaching all afternoon and assume she's still in bed."

"What about you, Lionel?" I said. "Can you say for sure that Molly has been upstairs all day?"

The boy shifted his feet. "I can say that I 'aven't seen 'er go out. I been in 'ere with these silly girls, learning my readin' so's I can better myself for when I become a Runner."

"Bring her downstairs," Mr. Lavender said with finality.

Miss Ashton hurried to obey.

Miss Lavender turned to her father. "You aren't going to take that poor girl into custody."

"I have to, Lydia," Mr. Lavender said.

I felt powerless. I could see exactly where the Bow Street man's thoughts were going. Molly could easily have slipped out while Miss Ashton was otherwise occupied, shot Mr. Nevill, and returned without anyone being the wiser.

Molly came downstairs clad in a dress with small flowers printed on it. Her dark curls were disheveled, and she yawned. But when her gaze met Mr. Lavender's, her brown eyes betrayed her fear.

Mr. Lavender was at his most official. "Molly, have you been upstairs in your room all afternoon?"

"Y-yes, why?"

"Do you have anyone who can bear witness that you've not left the Haven of Hope all day?"

"Well, everyone's been busy. It's not like anyone has been watching over me. Why are you asking these questions?"

"Father, please," Miss Lavender said.

"Molly, you'll need to come with me to Bow Street," Mr. Lavender said.

"Bow Street! Then you think Mr. Nevill is telling the truth? That I had a gun? I never did, I swear it!"

"Mr. Nevill is dead," Mr. Lavender said bluntly. "He was shot through the heart exactly like Mr. Jacombe."

"Dear God! And you think I killed two people!" Molly exclaimed. She burst into tears. Miss Lavender quickly put an arm around her.

I turned to the Bow Street man. "Cannot you see this girl is incapable of killing one person, much less two?"

"I am not in the business of judging people by their looks, Mr. Brummell. Come along now, Molly."

Mr. Lavender led the girl away, but not before his daughter pressed money into his hand with instructions that if Molly were taken to King's Bench Prison, she was to have a clean, private cell.

The four of us stood miserably after Molly and Mr. Lavender left. Miss Ashton took Lionel into the kitchen to fix some tea. The other girls went upstairs, no doubt to gossip about what had happened. Miss Lavender and I were alone in the classroom.

"What is our next move, Mr. Brummell?" Miss Lavender asked.

"I think we must go to Mrs. Hargrove."

"What are you thinking?"

"I am thinking that Mrs. Hargrove is someone who would have motive to kill both Mr. Jacombe and Mr. Nevill. Mr. Jacombe is Molly's father and the one responsible for Molly ending up without a place to live. He denies parentage, stops payments, and then is to fight a duel with the girl's betrothed."

"There's reason enough."

"Right. Then Mr. Nevill makes himself a target by going to Bow Street and planting the seed that Molly is the killer, not the lieutenant."

"Would Mrs. Hargrove have heard about that?"

"Oh, yes. Never, ever, underestimate the speed with which gossip travels through London, Miss Lavender. I could proclaim the newest shade of cloth to be unfashionable, and ten minutes later, tailors across Town would be grinding their teeth in frustration."

"So Mrs. Hargrove could have killed them both."

"Indeed. What we need to do is find out where Mrs. Hargrove was when Mr. Nevill was shot. Come to think of it, where was she the night Mr. Jacombe was shot? Can she provide an alibi for both herself and Mrs. Jacombe?"

"Let us go tomorrow and find out."

"Er, I cannot take you, Miss Lavender. Think, now, before you become insulted. What excuse would I give for having you with me?"

"True. It's not as if I were of the same station in life as you are, so we could pay a call together."

"Look, I have another idea. The killer has been sending me letters—"

"What!"

"Yes, another arrived today. Perhaps you could go to the back door of the Jacombe house and try to get a sample of Mrs. Hargrove's handwriting."

"I could say that I want her signature on a petition for the equality of the sexes."

"Excellent. Then we could meet at my house and discuss what we have found out. Say around three?"

"All right," Miss Lavender said.

"Try not to worry overmuch about Molly," I said, taking Miss Lavender's hand. It felt small and warm in mine. Very agreeable.

She looked down at our joined hands, then into my eyes. "I have confidence that together we can find the killer."

I raised her hand and pressed a kiss on her knuckles. I wondered if she would go out that night and bury another piece of the dress, another piece of her past.

I hoped she would.

22

Tuesday, I was once again admitted to the Jacombe house and shown to the green-and-ivory sitting-room after requesting to speak with Mrs. Hargrove.

"I thought you would want to know that Molly has been taken into custody by Bow Street," I said to the housekeeper in a solemn tone.

"I heard. Did she kill Mr. Nevill?"

"I do not believe she did. Do you, Mrs. Hargrove?"

"How should I know?"

"You are her mother."

"I gave birth to her, nothing more."

"So you care not whether she is in gaol."

"I cannot afford to care. I severed that tie long ago."

"Did you? I wonder. I wonder how a woman could know her daughter is in gaol under suspicion of killing two men— for you know that Mr. Nevill said he saw Molly with a gun that night at Vauxhall—and remain unaffected."

Mrs. Hargrove's impassive face was my answer.

"Where were you yesterday afternoon, Mrs. Hargrove?"

"Here at the house, overseeing the servants."

"The servants will vouch for your words?"

"Of course they will. I employ honest servants."

Was there nothing I could say that would draw an emotional response from the woman?

"What of the night Mr. Jacombe was killed? Where were you then?"

"Again, I was here at the house."

"You did not go to Vauxhall?"

"No. Mrs. Jacombe gave the servants the evening off so they could enjoy the gala evening at the Pleasure Gardens, but I remained here."

"Why?"

"In case Mrs. Jacombe needed anything."

"And did she?"

"No. I went to bed early with an improving book. She never rang for me. She is a courteous woman and knew I was here alone."

"How do you know she was here all evening?"

That seemed to ruffle her a bit. "Mrs. Jacombe would hardly have gone to Vauxhall, come home, and gone to bed, knowing her husband was murdered. She was sound asleep when the constables came to tell her. Besides, Mrs. Jacombe rarely leaves the house. She has been quite sheltered in her marriage."

Mrs. Hargrove was ever the loyal servant, I would give her that.

I tried once more for some sort of outburst. "So which one of them do you think committed these murders? Your daughter, her betrothed, or both of them?"

"I know nothing so cannot comment."

Feeling a strong wave of frustration, I thanked the house-keeper for her time. As she showed me upstairs where I could see Mrs. Jacombe, I thought of Miss Lavender. I hoped she would have better luck in obtaining a sample of Mrs. Hargrove's handwriting. Getting anything else out of the woman was about as easy as persuading Robinson to give Chakkri a kiss on the nose—and about as likely.

Upstairs, Mrs. Jacombe, a small figure on the sofa near the table containing her patent medicines, looked fatigued. That air of sadness surrounded her like a shroud. Her greyhound lay at her feet, while the physician, Doctor Trusdale, hovered nearby. Freddie sat in a chair, working some embroidery. A scene with a dog in it, I surmised. She looked lovely in a lilac gown, but her manner toward me was as distant as ever.

I bowed to Mrs. Jacombe. "I hope you do not mind me calling."

"Not at all, Mr. Brummell. I enjoy your company and know you are a dear friend of Frederica's."

The physician glowered a warning at me.

"How are you today, Mrs. Jacombe?" I asked.

"Doctor Trusdale is taking care of me," she replied in a low voice. "I am afraid I must not reflect positively on him, since I am not well."

"Now, Mrs. Jacombe, do not ever think that way. You have suffered a great shock and cannot be expected to be otherwise," soothed the doctor.

"Yes," she said in a sad voice, "it has all been a great shock. Now I understand the soldier accused of my husband's murder has confessed."

"He has," I said, a little surprised she did not know the whole story, that which involved Molly. But then had not

Mrs. Hargrove just told me that Mrs. Jacombe led a sheltered life? Perhaps they had kept the news about Molly from her. "The lieutenant's grandfather, Mr. Nevill, went to Bow Street and said that he had seen his grandson's betrothed, Molly, with a gun before the shooting."

Mrs. Jacombe pressed a hand to her chest. "Oh, dear."

Ignoring Doctor Trusdale's warning look, I went on. "Yes, now they have Molly in gaol as well, because yesterday afternoon, Mr. Nevill was shot through the heart exactly the way your husband was."

Instantly, I felt like a cad for blurting out this information. For Mrs. Jacombe gasped for breath like one about to have a heart seizure.

Freddie jumped from her chair to console her friend.

Doctor Trusdale rapidly placed drops from one of the medicine bottles into a glass with a little wine and urged his patient to drink. She did, and gradually her breathing returned to normal.

"I beg your pardon, Mrs. Jacombe," I said when she had settled. "I should not have spoken."

"No, you should not have," the doctor said, shooting me an angry look.

Mrs. Jacombe waved a handkerchief. "It is all right. Do not blame yourself, Mr. Brummell."

"If I could just ask one question before I take my leave. Was Mrs. Hargrove here in the house yesterday afternoon?"

"She was," Mrs. Jacombe confirmed. "Why would you want to know?"

Receiving yet another hostile glare from Doctor Trusdale, I dared not explain my suspicions. "No reason other than curiosity. I shall take my leave now. I hope your health improves, Mrs. Jacombe."

"Thank you, Mr. Brummell. You are most kind. Please call on us again."

"Your Royal Highness," I said, bowing low to Freddie.

"George, it is always pleasant to see you, even under these trying circumstances."

My heart sank a little more at those formal words, ones without a hint of warmth in them.

Doctor Trusdale followed me into the hall. I knew he was going to read me a lecture on upsetting Mrs. Jacombe, and I was correct.

No sooner had we traversed the bottom stair than he said, "Some men do not have great sensitivity of feeling, Mr. Brummell, and I can only assume you are one of them. I am forced to tell you that speaking of matters relating to her husband's death is upsetting, even dangerous, to Mrs. Jacombe. She is a fragile woman who has suffered a great loss."

"I understand, Doctor Trusdale. I have no wish to cause Mrs. Jacombe any further distress. It is merely that I want to find out who really killed her husband. I need to have the answers to certain questions, like the one I posed about Mrs. Hargrove's whereabouts."

"You do not think the soldier guilty, then?"

"No."

"I suppose you have a point, especially now that there has been another murder. The lieutenant could hardly have committed that one from gaol."

"I do not believe he killed either person."

The doctor ran a hand through his dark hair. "What a coil. You must see how it is my duty to protect Mrs. Jacombe from anything that could bring on an attack of nerves. Her heart is not strong. I fear for her."

"You have my word that I will only call on her again if it is absolutely necessary."

"Thank you."

I turned to go, then suddenly thought the physician might help me with another problem. "Er, Doctor Trusdale, forgive me if I overstep my bounds. No doubt you have people ask for your professional advice at the most unlikely of times."

He gave a slight smile. "Go ahead, Mr. Brummell."

"This is quite unusual, I am embarrassed to say."

"There is nothing I have not heard."

"The mother of two of my servants is staying in my house along with her pet piglet. The piglet has developed a rash. Mrs. Ed is in an uproar because she cannot procure something called Smith's Swine Salve here in London."

The doctor laughed. "Oh, they only make that in Dorset, but it is a simple enough compound." He drew a pad of paper from his pocket and wrote out the names and measures of some ingredients. "Have an apothecary make this up and give it to the woman. She will find it to be the very same thing as Smith's. Her piglet will shortly be in fine health."

I folded the paper and placed it in my pocket. "I am obliged to you, Doctor Trusdale."

"Happy to help. Just bear in mind what I said about Mrs. Jacombe."

I took my leave and started out for the nearest apothecary. Then I glanced at my pocket-watch and noted the hour lacked only ten minutes until three, the appointed time for me to meet Miss Lavender at my house.

I redirected my steps and arrived in Bruton Street just as Miss Lavender was about to knock on my door. I dismissed Robinson—his look plainly told me he did not approve of yet another visit from Miss Lavender—and took her into my bookroom.

"What did you find out?" she asked.

"Everyone was snug at the Jacombe house both the night of the murder in the Pleasure Gardens and yesterday afternoon. I still think Mrs. Hargrove is our chief suspect though, Miss Lavender. You would not believe the coldness of this woman."

"Yes, I would." She pulled out a piece of paper with a flourish. "It took some persuading, but I was able to get her to sign this petition."

I took the paper from her hand. At the top it said, "A Plea For The Streets Of London To Be Cleared Of Prostitutes."

"What a good choice. And this is her signature at the bottom. Let me get out my letters." I retrieved the two letters from the killer and compared the writing with that of Mrs. Hargrove. "Deuce take it."

"They don't match?"

"Well, it is difficult to say. The letters from the killer are printed, whereas Mrs. Hargrove has signed her name in a script writing."

"Let me see," Miss Lavender said. "You're right, it's next to impossible to tell. The handwriting of the killer looks deliberately printed in a block style that could be duplicated by anyone. Now what?"

"I shall think of something."

"While you're thinking, I want to go visit Molly and make certain she is as comfortable as possible, given that she's in gaol."

"Find out, if you will, whether they are going to release

the lieutenant, despite his confession, or if they plan to keep two people in gaol for the same murders."

"Very well." She turned to go, but I stayed her with a light touch on her shoulder. I angled my way in front of her. "I was wondering if you would accompany me tonight to a musical evening at Lord and Lady Perry's house. You know them, so I thought you would not feel uncomfortable. Please say yes."

She looked at me, and I hoped my grey gaze reflected the proper amount of desire for her company.

"There are bound to be Society people there, though, Mr. Brummell. Are you certain *you* would feel comfortable with me there?"

I reached out and brushed a dark red curl from her white skin. "I would be honoured."

She leaned closer to me. "In that case, I should like it very well indeed."

"I shall come for you—"

"At the Haven of Hope. No need to worry Father."

I chuckled. "I shall be there at eight."

Now at that moment, I felt compelled to conduct a bit of an experiment. You may recall me telling you how pleasant it felt to kiss Miss Lavender's lips. One cannot be absolutely certain of a sensation, I think, unless it is repeated with the same results.

Thus, I leaned down and brushed Miss Lavender's lips with my own. Just a light touch, you understand. Nothing scandalous.

Until I tasted the sweetness of her mouth and felt her response.

Then, er, well, the kiss I gave her was anything but proper.

Let us just leave it at that.

We were both rather breathless when it was over. Somehow we made it to the front door, where Miss Lavender went
on her way. I picked up my hat and my dog's head stick
and walked to the apothecary. I cannot report whom I saw
on the way or anything much other than the day was fine.
My head felt a trifle disordered from that kiss.

One might say it was something of a miracle then that,
as I was passing Doctor Trusdale's list of ingredients to the
apothecary, I noted the handwriting was the same block
print as the killer's.

❧ 23 ❧

The ballroom at the Perrys' Town house in Grosvenor Square was large and perfumed with the scent of hundreds of roses in a riot of colours. The ivory walls with their gilt-framed, floor-length mirrors reflected the selected assembly. At one end of the room, a pianoforte gleamed in the candlelight. Gilt chairs stood in rows, waiting for their occupants once the entertainment began.

At the other end, a trio of musicians anticipated their turn. I suspected that we would listen to a singer accompanied by the pianoforte first, then later there would be dancing. I said as much to Miss Lavender.

"I don't think I've ever been in such a grand room in my life," she said.

"Where did you tell your father you were going?"

"I didn't exactly say. I just went home, gathered this dress and some other things in a case, and left. Oh, I did find out that there are certainly no plans to release Molly just yet, even with Lieutenant Nevill's confession. The matter of who

killed Mr. Nevill is still up in the air. There are some at
Bow Street who believe Lieutenant Nevill killed Mr. Jacombe, then Molly killed Mr. Nevill to protect herself."

"I see. What a mess. But we shall contrive."

Miss Lavender's gaze flicked from person to person in the
room. "I confess I am a little nervous here."

"But you know the Perrys."

"They were most kind and gracious when they greeted
us."

I observed that despite her acquaintance with our host
and hostess, Miss Lavender did appear ill at ease. Her lashes
dropped at the approach of any stranger—and they were all
strangers to her except for the Perrys—and her slim white
fingers trembled on her crystal wineglass.

She certainly looked beautiful enough to grace any ballroom. Clad in a deep forest-green gown with a golden floral
pattern trimming the bodice, sleeves, and hem, and gold
leaves woven through her dark red curls, she was the beauty
of the room.

Lord Petersham, in company with Lord Munro as usual,
hailed us, and I performed the introductions.

"Charmed to meet you, Miss Lavender," Petersham said.
"Know your father a little. Bow Street man, isn't he?"

"Yes."

Munro's mouth puckered. His gaze raked Miss Lavender
from head to toe. He spoke not a word to the girl. To me
he said, "I see you are toying in Bow Street work in all
manners these days, Brummell."

Imbecile. I cut him a scathing look. "I want to see justice
done in the Jacombe murder case. I cannot believe Lieutenant Nevill guilty."

"Nonetheless, he's sure to be sentenced to hang by the

end of the week with all London crying for it," Munro went on. "Unlike some, the Lord Chief Justice is not a man to be diverted by anything," he finished, giving a pointed look at Miss Lavender.

I steered her away from them after telling Petersham I would see him at Watier's. I was indignant at Munro's thinly veiled insult to Miss Lavender.

As I introduced Miss Lavender to various people, the result was universal: a slight nod of the head, if anything. She was being snubbed. I overheard Lady Crecy say to a friend that I must have brought the girl here as some sort of jest. Luckily, I do not think Miss Lavender heard this cruel remark.

I felt terribly guilty. I, above anyone, should have known that the snobbery in Society would shut the girl out even if she appeared on my arm. In Society's eyes, it was a *mésalliance,* an undesirable match with one of lower social standing.

She felt it as well. "Mr. Brummell, while I know you meant well, it was a mistake bringing me here tonight. I do not belong at a *Beau Monde* entertainment. What's more, it's doing no good to your reputation to have brought me here, and since I know you live on your reputation—"

"Do not be tiresome, Miss Lavender," I said, trying to dismiss the effects of the atmosphere in the room. "I am honoured to escort you."

I wished desperately for the company of Lord or Lady Perry, whom I knew would be cordial to the girl, but they were occupied in greeting other guests.

At last salvation came in the form of the gruff Lady Salisbury. When I introduced her to Miss Lavender, she looked the girl up and down in quite a different way than Lord Munro had.

"I've heard of your father, John Lavender. He's reported to be a good man, one who tries for justice in this city where there is little."

"Thank you, my lady," Miss Lavender said, dropping a curtsey.

"And what do you do with your time?" the marchioness asked.

"I run a shelter for women called the Haven of Hope."

"Good for you. Someone's got to help out these poor girls running about the streets. Do you accept donations for your work?"

"Gratefully."

"Well, you can expect one from me. George, make sure you give me Miss Lavender's direction."

These words were said in the marchioness's usual gruff way, but her eyes told me a different story. Even she knew it was not appropriate for Miss Lavender to be in this company, but she is a true lady and would not cut any woman on my arm.

I admit I knew I should not have brought Miss Lavender, but my wish to spend time with her overclouded my judgment.

We sat through the singing of a fine tenor who entertained us with a variety of popular ballads, but at Miss Lavender's request, we took our leave before the dancing began.

In the hackney-coach on the way back to the Haven of Hope, I felt wretched and angry at the closed door that had clearly been shown to Miss Lavender.

She interrupted these maudlin thoughts. "Have you thought any more about Mrs. Hargrove as our chief suspect?"

"I almost forgot. We have another suspect."

"Who?"

"Doctor Trusdale, the physician. Quite by accident I obtained a sample of his handwriting. It was in the same printed, block style as the killer's."

"This is exciting news, but what motive could he have for killing Mr. Jacombe and Mr. Nevill?"

"I have thought about that. Doctor Trusdale has evidently served the Jacombe family throughout their marriage. He shows a fondness for Mrs. Jacombe that I believe crosses the line of the friendly family physician."

"Oh, my."

"Yes. He could have found out about some of Mr. Jacombe's nefarious activities and sought to protect Mrs. Jacombe by eliminating him. This would also pave the way clear for his own suit of the lady."

"Do you think he loves her, then?"

"I have only observed them together a few times, but yes, I do."

"Or the doctor could be writing the letters for someone else, Mrs. Hargrove or even Mrs. Jacombe," Miss Lavender said.

"Possibly. I had not thought of that. You have your father's powers of deduction, Miss Lavender."

"Thank you."

"Also, we must remember that Doctor Trusdale was involved in that bear-baiting scheme with Mr. Jacombe."

"Yes, and there might have been trouble there. Two men who would involve themselves in hurting animals cannot have much character."

"My feelings exactly. What I cannot understand is what motive Doctor Trusdale would have for killing Mr. Nevill."

"Do we even know if they were acquainted?"

"No, we do not. I think we need to learn more about Mr. Nevill."

"How are we—oh, never mind, I think I know how."

I smiled in the darkness of the coach. "I will make sure you are back at the shelter before I break into Mr. Nevill's room once more. That way, you cannot bear witness against me."

She laughed softly, making me want to take her into my arms.

But I felt I could not.

She must have felt the same way, for she left me with only a soft "Good evening."

Frustrated, I instructed the driver to take me to the end of the street, where I paid him and sent him on his way. With my dog's head cane, its deadly swordstick concealed in the tip, I waited to see if Miss Lavender was going to return to Mr. Jacombe's grave with another swatch of material from her dress.

Indeed, after some twenty minutes, she emerged from the shelter clad in the hooded cloak that hid her red hair.

I followed her the long way to St. George's graveyard and watched from a distance as she repeated the ritual. I felt a deep sense of sorrow now that I knew what the whole business was about. Perhaps by doing this, though, Miss Lavender would be able to rid herself of the demon of Mr. Jacombe.

After seeing her safely hail a hackney-coach to take her, I assumed, home to Fetter Lane, I turned my steps in the direction of Mr. Nevill's rooms.

This time, I was able to pick the lock rapidly and enter the darkened room.

The sitting-room already had a musty smell about it. I dared light only one candle to see my way around lest someone be alerted to my presence.

I began my search in the most logical of places: the heavily carved mahogany desk. Here was a collection of papers, some dating back as far as thirty years ago. After a good hour of sifting through receipts from various merchants, records of property bought and sold, and a note written to himself regarding the large amount paid in that banking deal, I felt entirely thwarted.

I closed one of the smaller desk drawers with what might be deemed more force than strictly necessary, when the wood caught on another paper. I pulled the drawer open again and lifted it out of its compartment. There in the back was the culprit. I reached in and pulled it out.

Scanning the contents, I could hardly believe what I read. The paper was an agreement between one Elsworth Nevill and Arabella Nevill, his son Harry's wife. The one he had told me was a heartless flirt who had left his son with a lover and fled to the Continent.

According to the paper I now held in my hand, that was not precisely the truth. Mr. Nevill had *paid* Arabella Nevill ten thousand pounds for her to leave England and never return. Nor was she to have any contact with her son, Nicholas Nevill. In addition, there was the matter of a diamond necklace in dispute. Conditions were set out where if Mrs. Nevill did indeed go against this agreement and return to England, Mr. Nevill would have Arabella Nevill prosecuted for the theft and subsequent sale of this family heirloom.

I sat back in the chair, hardly able to believe such perfidy on Mr. Nevill's part. And what of this Arabella Nevill? What kind of a woman agreed to such conditions? I remembered how Mr. Nevill had told me his daughter-in-law's actions had led to his son's death. Well, he had certainly had a part in it!

Disgusted, I threw the document aside and paced the room.

This still gave me no clues as to why Doctor Trusdale would kill Mr. Nevill. It just did not make sense.

The killer in this whole sorry mess was obviously remorseful; that was clear from the letters. But was he or she remorseful over the death of Mr. Jacombe or over the lieutenant being falsely accused? Assuming Doctor Trusdale was the killer and remorseful over the lieutenant, why kill the young man's grandfather?

I had no answers.

Picking up the candle from the desk, I went into the small bedchamber, thinking to give it a cursory look. The dressing-table revealed nothing; neither did the wardrobe.

The only thing unusual I found in there was a painting propped up against the back of the inside of the wardrobe.

Reaching inside, I pulled the painting from the wardrobe and laid it against the outside where I could see it. Holding the candle in front of it, I saw what appeared to be a family portrait.

Lieutenant Nevill, perhaps all of ten years old, sat between his mother and a man obviously his father. The resemblance was there. This must be the ill-fated Harry, I thought. The man who had no head for business nor good judgment when it came to a choice in wives.

I looked at the blond-haired female I assumed was Arabella Nevill. She was pretty, but no great beauty. Her figure was good, if this painting were to be of any measure. Oftentimes artists, at the request of their paying customers, softened the lines of the face, or subtracted unwanted pounds from a lady's figure.

One hand rested on the boy's left shoulder. Around Arabella's throat was a substantial diamond necklace, no doubt the one referred to in the agreement I had just read.

As I stared at the seemingly happy family portrayed in this likeness, I could not help but think of their fates.

The wife to leave her husband and son for money, safety from the threat of prosecution, and perhaps a lover to flee to the Continent with.

The father, a man literally destroyed by his wife's betrayal, who drank himself to death a year after she left him.

And finally the young man who at this moment sat in King's Bench Prison awaiting a certain death sentence.

No wonder Mr. Nevill did not have the painting on display and instead had it hidden.

About to replace it, I suddenly took another look at Arabella Nevill. I tilted my head. In my mind's eye, I added wrinkles to her face, another ten years to her features, and at least twenty pounds.

All of a sudden, she became the woman introduced to me at Mrs. Roucliffe's house as Angelica Nunn.

❧ 24 ❧

Wednesday morning, I gave Mrs. Ed the salve the apothecary had made up per Doctor Trusdale's instructions. While she looked at it dubiously, no doubt wondering if any London preparation could equal Smith's Swine Salve, she reluctantly took it and agreed to try it on Winifred.

Meanwhile, Chakkri seemed to be feeling the presence of another animal in the house. He kept to my bedroom and, of course, the dining-room where a shrimp might fall his way. I tried to speak with him about the matter.

"You know, Chakkri, old boy, Winifred is only here temporarily. And she is ill with a rash. Where is your sense of compassion? There is no need to keep yourself so rigid about the matter."

"Reow," he replied noncommittally.

"Between you and Robinson, I wonder how I ever have any peace in my own home."

"Reow."

"Well, in case you did not know, I have the devil of a

situation on my hands. Perhaps you could show a little sympathy. First Mr. Jacombe is killed, and now Mr. Nevill too has been shot through the heart. Bow Street has both Lieutenant Nevill and Molly in gaol. Lieutenant Nevill is sure to hang—God knows what they will do with Molly—unless I do something like produce the real killer for Bow Street. Do you not understand the gravity of the situation?"

Chakkri put both paws over his eyes.

"What do you mean by that, covering your eyes that way? I have noticed you have been doing that a lot recently. Is this your way of telling me you do not wish to have any part of my troubles? If so, I must say it is not very sporting of you. How would you like to be cut down in the prime of your life for a crime you did not commit, eh? That is what Lieutenant Nevill is facing."

The cat made no reply. What could he say to this, after all? Do you think him a sage?

Robinson entered the room. He held a handkerchief to his nose. "Sir, Mrs. Ed is down in the kitchens with the piglet. She has smoothed that salve all over the animal and placed him in the tub used for your baths."

"Good God. In my tub! Whyever did she do that?"

"I suppose she did not want a greased pig running about. We must be grateful for that much, I expect," Robinson intoned at his most sanctimonious.

"Make certain the tub is cleaned thoroughly before it is brought up for my bath. Which I am wanting now."

"I shall endeavour to do my best under these trying circumstances, sir."

Do I have to tell you that a considerable amount of time had passed before I left the domestic concerns of my home behind?

I was faultlessly groomed and attired in a Turkish-blue coat and light tan breeches when I set out for Doctor Trusdale's office in Chandos Street. I had one of the killer's letters in my pocket, along with the instructions for the apothecary that Doctor Trusdale had written.

The latter I had been able to persuade the chemist to return to me. I could not wait to hear what Doctor Trusdale would say when confronted with the two handwriting samples.

Later on, I planned to visit Mrs. Roucliffe and find out where "Angelica Nunn" was staying. I wanted to have a word with that woman, as well.

Arriving at Doctor Trusdale's office, I entered a reception area. A long counter stood as a barrier between visitors and the physician. A sandy-haired clerk with a thin, sallow face took my name and scurried off to announce my arrival.

Two doors stood behind the counter. One was open. This was the examining room, cluttered with steel instruments. I cringed a bit, thinking of the things that went on in there. The other door was closed, and that was where the clerk knocked and was admitted.

To my right was a staircase. I surmised that Doctor Trusdale lived above his office. The idea that I would like to survey the premises upstairs swept into my brain. This inspection of other people's property was becoming an alarming habit of mine, do you not think so? But how fruitful it usually turned out to be.

At last, the clerk returned and told me that Doctor Trusdale would see me. I was ushered in to the physician's office, where he sat in a leather chair behind a large desk.

"Mr. Brummell, I did not expect a visit from you. I am

afraid I am expecting a patient any moment. Is this in regard to your friend's piglet?"

"Not directly. Although it does involve the instructions you wrote out for the salve." I watched him carefully, noting that his hands gripped either side of his chair, as if he would rise at any moment and send me on my way.

"What is it, then? I am a busy man."

Without taking my eyes from his face, I withdrew the killer's letter from my pocket and tossed it on the desk. "Read this."

He scanned the few lines, then looked up at me, his eyebrows raised. "Who sent this to you?"

"That is what I am trying to determine." I placed the piece of paper with his handwriting down on the desk next to the note from the killer. "I thought you might be able to tell me."

He glanced only briefly at the words he had written. "Why should I know?"

"The handwriting on that letter is remarkably similar to your own, Doctor Trusdale."

A tense silence enveloped the room. Then the doctor relaxed back into his chair. "The handwriting is printed," he stated with an air of finality. "Many people print in a similar fashion."

"Perhaps. But I find it alarming that the handwriting of the killer should so closely match your own."

He rose, suddenly impatient and irate. "Are you accusing me of murder? I have taken an oath to save lives, not destroy them, Mr. Brummell."

I stood as well. "What was your relationship with Mr. Jacombe? You were business partners in a bear-baiting scheme, were you not?"

His face reflected surprise. "That was a long time ago. Jacombe convinced me to come in with him on the deal, but once I witnessed one of the events, I pulled out."

"Was Mr. Jacombe upset by the termination of your partnership?"

"No. We had been friends for many years. He did not care." He glared at me. "I am more than a little offended by this interrogation, Mr. Brummell."

"And I am offended at the very idea of an innocent young soldier sitting in King's Bench Prison with his life hanging in the balance."

"It has nothing to do with me. I feel sorry for the young man, regardless of whether or not he killed Mr. Jacombe, I assure you, but there is nothing I can do."

"Really? Let me tell you something else I have observed about you, Doctor Trusdale. I have noticed the *close* friendship you have with Mrs. Jacombe. I wonder at your very protective nature of another man's wife."

Red infused the doctor's face. "Why, I should think you would be very much aware of what it is like to feel protective of another man's wife. I have seen you with the Duchess of York."

That barb hit home. I lost my temper and dropped any formality. "The handwriting on your instructions to the apothecary matches that of the killer's note. That leads me to believe either you killed Mr. Jacombe or you are covering for Mrs. Jacombe or Mrs. Hargrove."

Doctor Trusdale's face was a mask of anger. "Get out of my office."

"You are in love with Mrs. Jacombe. You saw how her husband was treating her, knew of his affairs, his shady business dealings, and saw the way he kept her removed from

Society so that she might remain in ignorance of his true character, or lack thereof. So you went to Vauxhall that night and shot him."

"Winston!" the doctor shouted to the clerk.

"You can throw me out now, Doctor Trusdale, but I shall find out what happened."

"Then I have no need to worry about you any longer, Mr. Brummell, because it has nothing to do with me. Ah, Winston, this gentleman was just leaving."

"I hope you are telling the truth, Doctor Trusdale. But if you are not, rest assured I will know."

❦ 25 ❦

I left Doctor Trusdale's office and went directly to King's Bench Prison. I would see Mrs. Roucliffe soon, but the hour was still relatively early to call upon someone in her profession.

Molly was being questioned once again, the guard told me, so I was unable to see her. I sought Lieutenant Nevill's cell.

The young soldier had altered considerably from the last time I had seen him. His cheeks and chin were covered with stubble, his hair looked as if he had repeatedly thrust his fingers through it, and he wore the general air of one stretched to the very limit of his tether.

"Mr. Brummell! I am glad you've come. What are we to do? I cannot bear the thought that they have Molly here. I have not even been allowed to see her. What news have you?"

The guard closed the door to the cell behind me. "I can only imagine how you must be feeling, Lieutenant Nevill.

Molly is being questioned at the moment. I do know that Miss Lavender gave her father money for Molly to be kept in a private cell, as you are."

"That's a relief."

"May I offer my condolences on the loss of your grandfather?"

"Thank you," he replied, still in that agitated state. "I feel terrible that I can't muster much grief for the old man."

"That is quite understandable, given the circumstances. Once we have cleared your name and Molly's, you might find it in your heart to forgive him for bearing evidence against her."

"I expect you have the right of it. But who killed him? This is all an unbelievable tangle."

"I was hoping we could talk about that. Have you had any ideas as to who might have harboured a grudge against your grandfather?"

The lieutenant let out a short laugh. "He was ruthless in his business dealings, but I don't know that anyone would have been driven to murder him. He was shot through the heart, they say, so I assume it was done by the same person who killed Mr. Jacombe."

"Two suspects come to mind. One of them is Doctor Trusdale."

"Who?"

"He is Mrs. Jacombe's physician. I believe him to be in love with her. I have found out that Mr. Jacombe was a most immoral man in every sense of the word. In order to protect the woman he loves, Doctor Trusdale might have killed Mr. Jacombe. The death of a husband would also clear the way for him to pursue the widow."

"I see. But why would he kill Grandfather?"

I sighed. "That is what I was hoping you would tell me. Did you ever hear your grandfather mention his name?"

"No."

"Do you know the name of your grandfather's physician?"

"Yes. Doctor Cawley."

"So you know of no connection whatsoever between the doctor and Mr. Nevill?"

"None. You said you had two suspects?" the young man reminded, a strong measure of desperation in his voice.

I could appreciate how he must be feeling, with a trial that was sure to be the shortest on record, then the word of the Lord Chief Justice being the only thing between him and a hangman's noose.

Unless I could uncover the killer.

And we were running out of time. Again this morning *The Times* was full of news about the Jacombe killing and the Nevill killing. Molly's name was given in connection with the latter. *The Morning Post* went so far as to report that Lieutenant Nevill had confessed to the murder of Mr. Jacombe. I had probably only a day or two left before the Lord Chief Justice would act.

Though I was loath to do so, I must tell Lieutenant Nevill about Mrs. Hargrove. If there was anything he knew about the woman, I must be informed. I could try to avoid telling him that she was Molly's mother, but I thought the young soldier loved Molly enough to realise it would not be in her best interests to know of the relationship. He would protect her.

"Yes, there is a second suspect. The housekeeper at the Jacombe residence, Mrs. Hargrove."

A gleam of hope appeared in Lieutenant Nevill's blue eyes. "What of her?"

"What I am saying is confidential at the moment, you understand?"

He nodded.

"She bore Mr. Jacombe a child many years ago."

Lieutenant Nevill's brows came together. "Why would she kill him now? And why my grandfather?"

"Because Mrs. Hargrove is Molly's mother."

He drew in a sharp breath. "Are you certain?"

"Yes. I had hoped to keep the information from Molly, and will still do so if possible. Mrs. Hargrove is a cold woman who cares nothing for Molly. Or so it appears."

"As we all know, appearances can be deceiving."

"Exactly. Mrs. Hargrove is the only person I can determine who would have motive to kill both Mr. Jacombe and your grandfather."

"She would kill Jacombe because of what he'd done to her and possibly because he was to fight a duel with me, her daughter's betrothed," he said in dawning understanding.

"Precisely. Then, Mr. Nevill had to be eliminated because he pointed the finger at Molly. What it all comes down to is whether or not Mrs. Hargrove truly cares for her daughter. She certainly acts as though she does not."

"How can that be?" the lieutenant asked in wonder. "Molly is the dearest of girls."

"We cannot ever truly know what goes on in another's mind. I trust you will do with this information what you deem best in regards to Molly."

"I may not have much of a chance to do anything. I may not even get to kiss her goodbye before they hang me."

"Will you not consider retracting your confession? Can you not see that they have Molly in custody anyway?"

"If I recant my confession now, they are sure to convict Molly."

"Their evidence is not as strong without a living witness. Mr. Nevill may have given a statement to Bow Street saying he saw Molly with that pistol, but he is no longer able to face the Lord Chief Justice and convince him of the truth of his words."

The lieutenant shook his head. "I'll not put Molly in any more danger than she is already in."

There was one more piece of information I needed from the lieutenant, but I must tread carefully. "Is there no one else who might come to your aid? What of your mother?"

"Surely you jest. My mother has had nothing to do with me, not even a letter, since she left when I was but four-and-ten."

"I see. I know this is easy for me to say, but do try not to think of the worst. I have not ceased in my efforts to find out who committed these crimes. And I shall not until the killer is revealed."

"Thank you, Mr. Brummell," the soldier said in a low, defeated voice. "I owe you my life."

I hoped he would be alive long enough to continue to feel in my debt.

❧ 26 ❧

After I left King's Bench Prison, Ned and Ted carried me in my sedan-chair to the luxurious shop of Messrs. Rundell, Bridge and Rundell.

My visit to the jewellers had everything to do with Mrs. Roucliffe. I felt a little bauble might loosen her tongue and allow me to extract information about Arabella Nevill, or Angelica Nunn as she was calling herself.

Mr. Rundell greeted me at once. "Mr. Brummell, we are delighted to have you visit our shop. How may I serve you?"

Though Mr. Rundell is the soul of discretion, purchasing jewellery from those in need of funds, keeping quiet about a man's purchase for his latest mistress, and rarely dunning those who have not paid him, I could not count on any passerbys who might see me and report the fact around Town.

With Mr. Rundell's help, I made a hasty decision on some coral earbobs. They cost a bit more than I wanted to spend, but they were sure to please, being of that shade favoured by Mrs. Roucliffe.

While Mr. Rundell wrapped them up for me, I browsed the shop displays. A delicate gold heart suspended from a feminine chain caught my eye. I thought at once of Miss Lavender. The pretty filigree work was not so ornate as to offend her simple tastes, yet the golden piece was tastefully elegant.

"Here you are, Mr. Brummell," Mr. Rundell said. "I hope this gift will please, but if it does not, you have only to return it to me."

I thanked him and walked out of the shop. I told myself that a present of jewellery would not be appropriate for Miss Lavender. It flew in the face of the conventions for an unmarried gentleman to give an unmarried lady such a personal gift.

Ned and Ted stood at the ready with my sedan-chair.

I thought of how Miss Lavender's heart had been crushed by Mr. Jacombe, and how I hoped she was reclaiming it by burying the pieces of that dress and her memories.

Devil take the conventions.

I turned and walked back into the shop.

A short time later Ned and Ted carried me to Half Moon Street.

Mrs. Roucliffe was only too happy to receive me. "My *cher ami,* how happy I am that you have returned to visit! Sit by me," she invited, still adopting her French accent. Her dark hair was down, a riot of loose curls about her shoulders.

"Thank you for seeing me without, er, an appointment," I said, trying to keep my gaze from the clingy, diaphanous peach-coloured robe she wore that so closely followed her form at each move. Worse, I suddenly thought of Miss

Lavender in such a garment. I sat down abruptly.

"But you are always welcome here, Beau. I may call you Beau, may I not? And you will call me Cammie. For we are to be very close, like this," she said, moving close to me with her thigh pressed up against mine.

"I, er, thought you were under the protection of Lord Fogingham."

She leaned toward me and ran a finger under the top of my starched cravat. "He is a very nice man, but you are nicer, no?"

"Well, I—"

"This is a very complicated knot. What do you call it?"

"I do not have names or, rather I should say, a name, for this knot. Others like to create elaborate cravats and give them names, but I—"

"I understand. You like things simple. You are a man with much *savoir-vivre,* and as such, you have elegant, expensive tastes. That is why you have come to me. I think, though," she said, giving a little laugh, "that I could untie this knot, no?"

"No! I mean, that is not what I came here for."

Her red lips curved. "Are you sure about that?"

"Quite. I came to talk with you."

"Ah," she said in the manner of one who has dealt with such reluctance many times before and knows just how to overcome it. "We can talk, yes. I know lots of ways of talking. You like the baby talk, or maybe talk like this."

She whispered something in my ear that I do not wish to repeat to you. No, no matter how much you insist. Gentlemen do not repeat such things.

I tried to ease away from her. "I wish to speak about Angelica Nunn."

Her expression changed. "You like blondes? And she is older than me. I am very hurt that you would prefer her to me."

"You misunderstand."

She crossed her arms across her chest. "I don't think so," she said, the French accent slipping.

"Really, I simply want her direction—"

"So that you can go to her instead of stay here with me."

I had to play the game. "She reminds me of someone else. Someone I cannot have."

She softened. "Ah, an unrequited love."

"That is it."

She suddenly began to cry. "How terrible to love and not have it returned. Poor, dear Beau."

I produced my handkerchief and offered it to her. She took it, glancing at the double *B*'s initialed in the corner. Wiping her streaming eyes, she said, "I could make you forget her, you know. Who is it?"

"I cannot say." Which was true.

"A man of discretion." She blew her nose and pocketed the handkerchief. "And you say that Angelica reminds you of her."

"Actually, I am not sure. That is why I need her direction. So that I might see her and know."

She tapped a finger on the lapel of my coat. "I'm not sure I should tell you. It might be better for you not to be constantly reminded of this love you cannot have."

"I beg you will allow me to be the judge of that. Here, I have brought you something." I pulled out the box containing the coral earbobs and handed it to her.

"Oh! They are charming," she cried when she opened the lid. She leaned over and kissed me on the cheek. Then she got up and went to stand in front of a looking-glass so that she might admire them on herself.

I rose. "Have you known Mrs. Nunn long?"

"No, not at all. We met in the Park one day during the last Season. She had just arrived from Belgium, I think it was, and needed a protector." She turned from the mirror. "How do they look?"

"Very nice. They are perfect for you."

She laughed. "But then how could you, the Arbiter of Fashion, bring me something other than perfection?"

"You are very kind."

She walked over to me and placed her hands on the knot of my cravat. "What a shame to have this handsome figure wasted on such as Angelica. But perhaps you'll find you don't care for her after all."

"I will not know that until I see her again."

She pouted, then scrawled a direction in Bloomsbury on the back of one of her peach-coloured cards.

❦ 27 ❦

Lionel opened the door to me at the Haven of Hope around five that afternoon. His worried gaze met mine. I tried to adopt an air of confidence, though I was feeling anything but certain all would turn out well in this situation. In fact, as each hour went by, I doubted my ability to bring the real killer to justice before an unspeakable mistake on Bow Street's part could cost the lieutenant his life.

"How are you today, Lion?" I asked.

He turned and glanced down the hallway after closing the door behind me. "I'm that worried over Miss Lavender. She sits and stares at nothin' sometimes. I never seen 'er do the like. She's always been busy doin' somethin'. But 'ere lately, she's all drawn into 'erself."

I thought I could understand. Miss Lavender was going through the ordeal of letting the memories of what Mr. Jacombe did to her cease their control over her. It was no wonder that she was thoughtful and quiet.

However, I could not tell Lionel any of that. "I believe

her to still be disturbed by the fact she witnessed the death of Mr. Jacombe. Not to mention the incarceration of both Lieutenant Nevill and Molly. It is only natural that she be worried."

"And me, too?"

"Of course. You care for Miss Lavender."

"She prob'ly saved my life. At the very least she took me off the streets."

"Well then, halfling, you have your answer. Do not be overset. All is not lost." Yet.

"I expect you came to see 'er."

"Yes, though I always enjoy seeing you. Have you worked on tying your cravat?"

"I confess I 'aven't."

"That is all right. When this is over, we shall practice. I shall bring you to my house. I have plenty of linen you can work with."

Robinson would have to be given the afternoon off the day I brought the boy over, I thought. Can you imagine what the fussy valet would say about Lionel and my good linen?

The boy grinned. "That sounds good."

I left him to his studies and knocked on the door to Miss Lavender's office. A call to come in prompted me to open the door and enter.

Miss Lavender sat behind her desk, spectacles on her nose, going over a ledger.

"Mr. Brummell, I've been half waiting for you all day. Come and sit down." She removed her spectacles and indicated a chair across the desk from her.

"Thank you. How are you today?"

"Worn to the bone from my evening at the Perrys'," she said with a smile.

"I am glad you can make light of the awful way those people treated you. I am ashamed of them."

"Don't concern yourself with the matter. We have more important things to discuss."

"Yes. First tell me your news. Has your father said anything about a trial date?"

Miss Lavender looked grim. "I'm afraid he has. The trial is set for Friday morning. The word around Bow Street is that if the lieutenant is convicted, the Lord Chief Justice could sentence him to hang Saturday morning at eight."

"Good God! I knew things were coming to a crisis point, but to actually hear the date and know we have only a matter of tonight and tomorrow . . . I take it they will not release Molly?"

"Not until after the trial. Tell me what you've found out about Doctor Trusdale."

"Not much. I confronted him with the letter from the killer, placed alongside a sample of his own handwriting. He completely denied having written the letter. He said that many people's block style of handprinting is similar. I confess I must agree with him."

"What about his motive to protect Mrs. Jacombe?"

"I am certain he is indeed in love with her. I feel there is clearly a motive for him to have killed Mr. Jacombe. The problem is Mr. Nevill. I can find no connection whatsoever between the two men."

"I take it you searched Mr. Nevill's rooms last night after dropping me off."

No need to mention I had followed her to Mr. Jacombe's grave first, I thought. "Yes, I did go through Mr. Nevill's rooms. There was absolutely nothing there to link him to Doctor Trusdale."

"Faith, I don't know where all this is leading."

"I did find something of interest, however, in Mr. Nevill's rooms."

"What? Pray God it will help Molly and her young man."

"Inside the wardrobe in Mr. Nevill's bedchamber there was a portrait. A family portrait."

She looked bewildered. "How can that help?"

"I am not saying it can. But what was of interest was the likeness of Lieutenant Nevill's mother, Arabella. Recall that his mother allegedly abandoned the family and fled to the Continent with a lover."

"When was this?"

"When the lieutenant was but four-and-ten. His father drank himself to death within a year. At any rate, when I was going through the papers in Mr. Nevill's desk, I came upon a document. It was written up as an agreement between Mr. Nevill and Arabella Nevill. He paid her ten thousand pounds to leave the country and never return."

Miss Lavender drew a sharp breath. "How infamous. To send a mother away from her child. Was she a bad woman?"

"Evidently Mr. Nevill thought so. There was also the matter of a diamond necklace. It was referred to in the document as a family heirloom. Apparently Arabella sold it without permission."

"Oh, my."

"There is more. When I saw the likeness of Arabella in the family portrait, I thought she looked vaguely familiar. When I added years, wrinkles, and some weight to her, I knew for certain that I had seen her."

"Here in London?"

"Yes."

"But I thought you said the agreement prevented her from returning."

"It did. Which makes it imperative that we find out if the woman I saw is Arabella and how long she has been back in London."

"Where did you see her?"

Here was a bit of an awkward situation. For I would have to tell Miss Lavender that I had seen her at Mrs. Roucliffe's. I cleared my throat.

"A lucky encounter, actually," I said, trying to stall. "She was introduced to me as Angelica Nunn, but I believe her to be Arabella Nevill."

"I see. Who introduced you?"

Oh well. "Mrs. Roucliffe, the courtesan you saw me talking with at Gunter's that day."

Miss Lavender bridled like a dowager of sixty years. "Was Mrs. Nunn in company with Mrs. Roucliffe in the Park? Or where exactly did this take place?"

My throat felt dry, I wished for a large glass of Chambertin. Or any wine, actually. "At Mrs. Roucliffe's house."

Miss Lavender's green gaze held mine. A flush had stolen up over her throat and face. A moment or a thousand passed.

"I was at Mrs. Roucliffe's for perfectly innocent reasons."

"There is no need to explain yourself to *me*, Mr. Brummell."

"Now, Lydia, there is no need to take that tone."

"I have not given you leave to use my Christian name."

"Very well, Miss Lavender, please allow me to explain."

"I'm listening."

"That day at Gunter's when I was with you and Lionel, I made an appointment to see Mrs. Roucliffe. I wanted to find

out what she knew of Mr. Jacombe. I had been told by Lady
Salisbury, the marchioness you met last night, that Mr. Jacombe had tried to set up Mrs. Roucliffe as his mistress."

"Contemptible man. Did his lust know no bounds?"

"One cannot assume anything where Mr. Jacombe is concerned, it seems. But to return to Mrs. Roucliffe. I visited
her the next day. She told me that she had refused Mr.
Jacombe's offer of protection, refused the house he had let
for her, refused his money, all because she sensed a vein of
cruelty in him."

"A smart woman."

"Indeed. It was when I first arrived at Mrs. Roucliffe's
house that I met Mrs. Nunn. She and Mrs. Roucliffe are
friends. Mrs. Nunn was on the point of leaving when I arrived."

Miss Lavender relaxed. "I see. And from that brief meeting you recognised her in the portrait?"

"Yes."

"You are clever, Mr. Brummell."

I felt a glow of pride. And relief that she no longer seemed
angry with me. "Thank you. Earlier today I returned to Mrs.
Roucliffe's. She gave me Mrs. Nunn's direction in Bloomsbury."

Miss Lavender leaned forward eagerly. "What do you propose we do?"

"I think we need to confront Mrs. Nunn. My mind has
been intrigued by several possibilities where she is concerned. Mrs. Roucliffe said she met her in the Park one day
and helped get her a protector."

"She could have been in London watching her son and
seen events unfold."

"Possibly. We have a case here with two mothers—Mrs.

Hargrove and Mrs. Nunn, or Mrs. Nevill I should say—who may not care two straws for their children. On the other hand, I think it would be worth confronting Mrs. Nunn."

"Molly has some sketches she drew of Lieutenant Nevill. We could show her those and play on her emotions."

"Excellent. But I think we must tread carefully. A woman like Arabella Nevill is no fool. Let me go in alone, flatter her. When we see what sort of place she is living in, we can devise a means for you to be nearby listening."

"That way I can be a witness if she says anything incriminating."

"Precisely." I smiled at her. "Miss Lavender, your father must be in ignorance of the intelligence of his daughter; else he would have you working at Bow Street."

"What fustian," Miss Lavender murmured, but she lowered her lashes in pleasure at the compliment nonetheless.

"Can we agree on a time? I would say not too early in the morning in case Mrs. Nunn's protector is still with her, but not so late that she might be receiving him as a caller."

"What about one of the clock?" she asked.

"Excellent. Now I must take my leave so that I might change clothing for the evening. I am going to visit the Prince of Wales and see if there is any possibility he might change his mind and intercede on Lieutenant Nevill's behalf."

"I wish you good luck," she said, rising.

I rose as well and reached for her hand. I placed a brief kiss on her knuckles. "We need all the luck we can get, since we only have one more day before the trial."

✻ 28 ✻

The Rose Satin Drawing Room at Prinny's Carlton House may have a turquoise-and-green carpet, but the walls, draperies, sofas, and chairs are all done in the colour that gives the room its name.

Several large crystal chandeliers hang from the ceiling, which has squares of paintings around its oval gilt-trimmed frame.

I entered the room through the white-and-gold double doors to find the Prince in company with several male guests: Lords Petersham and Munro, Victor Tallarico, Count Boruwlaski, and unfortunately, Sylvester Fairingdale.

The company had done with dinner and were working hard to amuse themselves. A table for cards had been set up, but the Prince was not playing.

Instead, he was talking to the dwarf, John, Count Boruwlaski, while the latter stood on a Louis XIV table.

"Brummell!" the Prince called upon seeing me. "Just the man we need to entertain us with some *bon mots*."

I bowed. "I am afraid, sir, that I have come on a serious matter."

"Still trying to help your young friend escape the noose at Old Bailey?" Fairingdale crooned. "I fear it's a lost cause. Poor Brummell. You saved the man once, but you won't be able to do it again."

I ignored him and kept my gaze on the Prince. "Sir, I have come on behalf of Lieutenant Nevill."

"He's the one who's going to swing on Saturday morning, isn't he," the Count asked. "I thought you said you'd take me to watch, your Royal Highness."

Appalled, I could only stare at the Prince. Had he not asked me to find out who the real killer was? Now he was ready to watch the soldier hang?

"Now, John," the Prince said, addressing the Count, "I said we would see if it could be worked into the royal schedule."

"Egad," said Petersham. "Is it to be a public hanging?"

"I never attend those. Such a crush of common people," Munro pronounced.

"Are things so bleak for Lieutenant Nevill, Brummell?" Tallarico asked. "I thought certainly events would change to his benefit. Why, when I was speaking of the matter with the Royal Duchess yesterday, she assured me that something would be done to spare him."

I did not know whom I wanted to throttle first. Fairingdale for being his usual ugly self, or Tallarico for being his usual charming self when it came to Freddie.

I addressed the Prince. "Sir, we cannot stand by and let Lieutenant Nevill be hanged for a crime he did not commit."

"How are you so sure he didn't do it?" the Count asked.

"Because I know the man's character."

"But you didn't think he'd wager again when you let him off the hook regarding his debt at Watier's and yet he did. Else he wouldn't be in this mess," Fairingdale said.

"He had a purpose in gaming: to gain funds to marry the girl he loves."

"And he just as well had a purpose in ending poor Mr. Jacombe's life: to avoid the duel," Fairingdale said.

"I have looked into the matter. Mr. Jacombe was not the model of propriety he appeared to be," I said.

"Oh, do tell us all the details," the Count encouraged, jumping up and down on the fine table. No wonder Prinny treated him like a child. He acted like one.

"There is no time. Sir, is there nothing you can do to help? Ask Bow Street to set back the date of the trial at the very least."

Prinny looked skeptical. "I don't have any governing powers. I can't interfere with Bow Street."

"But your friend, Jack Townsend, at Bow Street—"

"This isn't in his control. It's one of the biggest scandals London has seen in ages. Only the Lord Chief Justice at King's Bench Prison has power over this. I must leave matters to him, else it looks like he does not have royal favour and England has no independent judiciary."

I could not argue with that. Well, I could, but it would be a waste of breath.

Frustrated, I stayed for a little while, but then made an excuse and took my leave.

Back home in Bruton Street, Robinson waited for me with complaints about Mrs. Ed.

"Sir, how much longer will she stay? André is upset as well as me. She has overturned his kitchen," Robinson said, handing me my nightclothes.

"She has only been here a week."

"One week and one day," Robinson corrected.

"What would you have me do, throw her out?"

Robinson looked hopeful.

"Leave me now, and wake me at ten if I am not already up."

"Very good, sir. Sleep well. I hope the sounds of pig squeals do not awaken you during the night." Robinson swept from the room with the clothes I had worn that day, leaving me alone with Chakkri.

The cat studied me with interest.

I poured myself a small snifter of brandy and crawled into bed.

Immediately Chakkri presented himself for a petting session.

I indulged him. What else could I do, I ask you?

"We are in deep trouble, Chakkri," I said, stroking his fawn-coloured body from head to tail.

He purred.

"You are not listening. We have only tomorrow before the trial. If Miss Lavender is correct, and I am sure she is, the Lord Chief Justice will make quick work about hearing the evidence, then sentence the lieutenant to be hanged on Saturday. Unless a miracle occurs."

The cat turned his rear to me and walked down to the end of the bed.

"Did you not hear me? That young soldier is going to die on Saturday. Bow Street has done nothing, believing they have the killer in hand. It is all up to me."

The cat found the centre of the bed, turned around twice, lay down with his chin on the bed, and put both his paws over his eyes.

I swallowed some brandy and eyed him. "Just what is the meaning of this performance? I swear you grow more peculiar by the day. Is there some reason why you do not wish to look at me? Have your meals not been served promptly? Has your sand tray not been kept meticulously clean? Have you not enough birds to look at from the windows? Why are you covering your eyes with your paws?"

But Chakkri spoke not a word. Devil.

I gave up trying to understand him.

Instead, I drank the rest of my brandy while contemplating how I might force a confession from one of the suspects prior to the trial on Friday.

Because once the trial was over, the lieutenant's fate was sealed.

Arabella's house was a paltry affair situated next to a gin shop. I met Miss Lavender outside at one of the clock on Thursday, feeling as if each minute that ticked by brought the lieutenant closer to his conviction and execution.

"We are in luck," she said in a low voice. "There are windows open on the ground floor."

"Yes, I will have to arrange it so she receives me in that particular room," I said, admiring the light blue gauzy gown Miss Lavender wore. And the woman in it.

Then I frowned at the idea of her travelling about without any maid. But she was the most independent female I had ever known. No one would ever be able to persuade her to go about escorted. Perhaps I could convince her to carry a pistol. I would have to speak to her about the matter.

"I'll wait here beside this window," she said.

I looked up and down the street. At least it was a quiet

neighbourhood. Still, I did not like the idea of Miss Lavender loitering about.

Just then, we heard two female voices from inside the house.

"And clean up that mess in the bedchamber. Mr. Parker was in a temper last night. He made me throw that blue-and-white pitcher at him."

"Yes, ma'am."

Miss Lavender looked at me. She spoke in an urgent voice. "I heard every word clearly. We could not hope for better. Let's get on with it."

"Very well. Mind yourself out here, and call out if you need me."

She placed one hand on her hip. "Mr. Brummell, I've been taking care of myself now for many years. I don't need a keeper."

I turned without a word and applied the brass door knocker with perhaps a trifle more force than I would normally use.

A harried maid in a dirty apron opened the door. Her grey hair was coming out of its knot and her face was covered in smallpox scars.

"George Brummell to see Mrs. Nunn," I said, handing her one of my cards.

She looked me up and down and then admitted me to a tiny hall. On a scratched table, a vase of wilted flowers seemed to echo the shabbiness of the house.

The maid went directly into the room at the right, the one where the windows were open. I just barely kept myself from cheering.

Not more than a few seconds passed before the maid reappeared and motioned for me to go inside.

I crossed the threshold and took in my surroundings slowly, making sure that I observed the windows last. It was a small sitting-room with a chintz sofa in greens and pinks and two green chairs. Faded paper in a moss-green colour covered the walls.

Arabella reclined on the sofa in a very low cut ivory-coloured gown. The sofa was positioned a few feet from the windows.

"Come in, Mr. Brummell. How perfectly lovely to see you," she cooed.

Drunk, I thought immediately. Her speech was slurred. How fortunate for me. Finally things might go my way.

She held a glass in one hand, but put it down very carefully, the way one does when one is inebriated, on a low table before rising unsteadily and extending one plump hand for me to kiss.

"You are very kind to receive me, Mrs. Nunn," I said, brushing the back of her hand with my lips.

Gin. She smelled of gin. She was probably the shop next door's best customer.

She turned her hand in mine and held it, leading me to the sofa.

"Sit here with me where we can have a comfortable coze. Did Cammie tell you how much I admired you the day we met?"

My gaze fell to the expanse of wrinkled flesh above the bodice of her gown. "Yes," I lied. "I wanted to get to know you better. In fact, I think I know one of your secrets."

She smiled in a suggestive way and pulled me closer to her on the sofa. I resisted the urge to jump up and move to one of the chairs. If this was to go the way I wanted, I must appear to be interested in the woman. And I was. Just not in the way she thought.

"Ooooh, I've got lots of secrets. A woman without secrets would hardly be worth knowing. And you've come at just the right time, Mr. Brummell, or may I call you Beau?"

"Please do."

"You can call me Angelica. My protector, Mr. Parker, and I had a disagreement last night. I don't know that I want to see him again. He's short for one thing, and thinks too much of himself for another," she said and frowned. She reached for her glass and took a long swallow. "I need a gentleman. Someone like yourself. Would you like a drink?"

"No, thank you."

"Not a drinking man, are you? That's good. Mr. Parker could get quite demanding when he drank. Of course, he is always demanding, and he smells bad too. You look like the sort who would treat a lady well."

"About that secret—"

She giggled, then whispered, "Yes, let's talk about secrets the way lovers do." She leaned close to me. The smell of gin was almost overwhelming.

"You have a son, do you not?"

She drew back. Her face changed. She looked unsure, wary, but the gin had worked in her brain, and she was confused. "What makes you think so?"

"I knew Mr. Elsworth Nevill slightly. He had a family portrait displayed over the mantel." I watched the words sink in. It would not do to antagonize her. "You have not changed at all," I said, adding another lie to the pile.

Then she shrugged a shoulder. "He was a nasty old man, Elsworth Nevill was. Didn't really like women. He despised his own wife. I think that's what sent her to an early grave."

"I expect you did not want a similar fate," I said in a conversational tone. She would not be speaking to me this way sober, I thought. This was a shrewd woman, I reminded myself.

"No, I did not." Another swallow of gin. "He came between me and Harry, my husband, you know."

"How so?"

A flare of anger shone in her dull eyes. "Always telling Harry whenever I had a little on the side. I ask you, is it not common for a woman to take lovers once she's given her husband an heir?"

"I believe that to be rather common," I said, sure she would not catch what I really meant by that statement.

She did not. "You are a reasonable man. Yet old Nevill never could shut his mouth about me. Turned my Harry against me. Told him I cost too much, that I was running through all the family money. What's money for, if not to be spent?"

"I am sure I do not know."

"He paid, though. I made him pay."

I thought of the document where Mr. Nevill had given Arabella the sum of ten thousand pounds to leave England. "But now here you are in London. Have you seen your son?"

"Nicholas? No, that's all in the past."

"His name has been in the newspapers, you know. He is accused of killing someone."

Her brows came together. "I heard something about that."

I studied her carefully, then reached in my pocket and withdrew the sketch of Lieutenant Nevill that Molly had done. "I thought you might want to see this."

I unfolded the likeness of her son. Arabella Nevill looked at it briefly, then took another drink. "Did he kill that man like they say he did? I never knew the child very well. He was always away at school or in the care of a governess."

"I do not believe he killed Mr. Jacombe, no. There was to be a duel between them the following day. Your son is no coward, Arabella. He would not have murdered the man he was set to fight."

"Maybe that old horror, Elsworth Nevill, did it. It would be the only decent thing he ever did in his life."

"He would not even bail his grandson out of gaol when he had the opportunity."

Her face turned an ugly red then. "That's old Nevill for you, the squeeze-purse. But I made him give me money to go away, and then when I came back, I made him give me more."

I barely refrained from gasping. Arabella Nevill had been blackmailing Mr. Nevill! Of course. She returned to England in need of funds and went right to him, most likely threatening to go to Lieutenant Nevill and tell him everything about that document. How his own grandfather had paid to keep his mother away. Not to mention the disgrace of having a courtesan as a daughter-in-law.

She was becoming more and more surly and angry, the way a drunk can, as she thought about Elsworth Nevill. I wanted to use it to my advantage to learn everything I could.

"So Mr. Nevill knew you were back in London and paid you to stay way from your own son."

"Yes," she said. "He didn't think me suitable to be the boy's mother. That was all at first."

She had drunk so much gin, I was afraid she was not

making sense any longer. "You mean when you went away the first time?"

"No, I mean when I came back. At first Elsworth gave me money to keep away from Nicholas. Then he stopped."

"Why would he do that?" I said in the voice of a confidant.

She laughed bitterly. "That's what I demanded of him the night I went to his rooms."

A chill ran through me. For a moment I could not speak. I remembered Miss Lavender was outside and prayed that she could hear every word of this.

In the most casual of voices I said, "What good reason did he give you for ceasing payments?"

"No good reason at all! He was furious that I came to him. He said that it would do Nicholas good to see the kind of woman I was. That then maybe he wouldn't marry whoever it is he is supposed to marry."

"What did you do then?"

"I argued with him. I threatened to go to Nicholas and tell him everything. All about how Elsworth had paid to send me away. I asked him how he thought his grandson would feel, knowing that his grandfather had *paid* his mother to leave England."

She took another drink and wiped her mouth with the back of her hand. I remained silent.

"He grew furious then, told me he'd send me to hell this time instead of just the Continent. He picked up a pistol and started waving it about."

I dared not say anything. She was caught up in remembering. I did not want to break her flow of thoughts.

"I told him he didn't have the gumption to kill me, that

if he did, he would have done it years ago. I demanded he write me a draft on his bank."

She tilted her head. "Then, suddenly, he pointed the pistol straight at me. For the first time, I was afraid. I lunged for the pistol and forced it toward him just as he pulled the trigger. Imagine that. He killed himself, really."

❦ 30 ❧

"*I was only* defending myself," Arabella went on.

Keep her talking, I thought, hoping Miss Lavender had heard the confession and had run for a constable. "Mr. Nevill was a most unpleasant man."

She brandished her drink, causing the liquid to slosh over the top. "He made a big fuss over my selling a diamond necklace that belonged to me. Said he'd go to the authorities. I ask you, since when is it illegal to sell one's own property?"

"I see your point. But as to Mr. Nevill's death, I feel you should tell Bow Street what happened. Do you know they are holding your son's betrothed, Molly, as a suspect?"

She pouted. "Let's not talk of this unpleasantness any longer. Let's talk about us instead."

"What about Mr. Jacombe?" I asked, with the frail hope that she might have killed him as well.

"The man my son supposedly shot? What about him?"

"Did you know him?"

"Never heard of him in my life before I saw his name in the newspaper in connection to Nicholas. What was it, cards they argued over? Men can be so silly."

A fierce knocking on the front door startled her. "I do hope that's not Mr. Parker. I've decided I'm done with him and his dramatic scenes."

The frightened maid admitted Miss Lavender and two constables. They were both beefy men, one so thickly muscled he looked as if he would pop out of his clothing.

The more muscular constable took charge. "Are you Arabella Nevill?"

Arabella rose unsteadily to her feet. "Yes."

"We have two witnesses here who've heard you confess to the killing of Elsworth Nevill," the constable said.

Arabella looked from Miss Lavender back to me. "You tricked me, Mr. Brummell. How did you know I'd killed him?"

"I assure you, I did not know until you told me," I said.

At that moment, a harried Mr. Lavender entered the room and was rapidly informed by the second constable as to what had transpired. Mr. Lavender scribbled a few lines in his ever-present notebook, glancing up occasionally at Arabella.

That woman was fast becoming sober. "All I was doing was defending myself, I tell you. It was an accident, really. Elsworth took out the pistol and pointed it at me!"

Mr. Lavender spoke: "You'll have ample opportunity to tell the court your story. Where were you on the night Theobald Jacombe was killed?"

"That was the night of the grand gala at Vauxhall, I remember from the newspapers. Mr. Parker, my friend, and I stayed here all evening. He didn't want to go out."

"What is his direction?"

Arabella gave a number in Jermyn Street.

"Right now, these constables are taking you into custody for the killing of Elsworth Nevill," Mr. Lavender said after marking down Mr. Parker's direction.

As the head constable reached for her, Arabella swiftly turned around and slapped me across the face. The blow stung.

"Trollop!" Arabella cried out at Miss Lavender.

The constables led her out of the house, protesting and swearing all the way.

Mr. Lavender, Miss Lavender, and I were left standing in the sitting room, the maid nowhere in sight.

"The two of you have been busy," Mr. Lavender said, his expression telling me he was not pleased at my involvement.

"You can release Molly from prison now that we have Nevill's real killer," I said.

Mr. Lavender pointed his finger at me. "Don't you be telling me what to do. You've meddled enough."

"Father, how can you call it meddling, when all we did was uncover the truth!" Miss Lavender exclaimed.

"And you, Lydia," Mr. Lavender rounded on his daughter. "The man that came for me said you'd been standing outside the window, listening to everything. Where is your sense? You could have been accosted, loitering about like that."

Miss Lavender's eyes sparked. "I've more sense than you have in this case, Father. You've held poor Molly and not even tried to find out what happened."

Mr. Lavender threw up his hands. "I can see I won't be able to reason with either of you."

"Will you have Molly released?" I asked.

"Yes, I'll see to it now, since I'm not getting anything

accomplished here. Lydia, I'll escort you back to the Haven of Hope."

"No, Father, I have things to discuss with Mr. Brummell."

At these words, the Bow Street man flashed me a look of fiery anger. He shook his head vehemently and stomped out of the house.

"His pride is hurt," Miss Lavender said.

"Perhaps. Let us go outside and hail a hackney," I said.

We walked out into the July sunshine to the end of the street, where we quickly found a willing vehicle.

Once settled inside, she said, "We've been looking at this whole thing as if the same person killed Mr. Jacombe and Mr. Nevill. It appears we were wrong."

"Yes, a devilish coil. Even I cannot believe that Arabella killed Mr. Jacombe. There is no connection between the two. Since she was, ahem, otherwise occupied the evening of the Vauxhall gala, I cannot think she would even have learned of the proposed duel, no less been at the Pleasure Gardens."

"True. Now what?"

"We are back to who killed Mr. Jacombe, that is what. And if we do not find out who the murderer is in short order, that young man's life is over."

❧ 31 ❧

At the Haven of Hope, we sat over cups of tea in Miss Lavender's office. She was behind the tattered desk. I sat in the more comfortable of the two upholstered chairs opposite. Miss Lavender had tried to brighten the room with a bowl of yellow roses. They sat on the edge of the desk, their fragrance perfuming the air.

We had sent Lionel down to King's Bench Prison to escort Molly home, certain that she would be released.

"Perhaps with Molly out of danger, Lieutenant Nevill could be persuaded to retract his confession," Miss Lavender said.

"One would think. I shall go to him in the morning before the trial starts and try to convince him. But we cannot count on him doing so, nor can we count on the court believing him. We must force the killer's hand today."

"Those letters you've received. They show the killer has some sympathy for Lieutenant Nevill," Miss Lavender mused.

"Yes. But not enough sympathy to come forward."

"Should we show the letters to Father now? At this point, surely he will believe you."

I raised a skeptical brow. "In case it has escaped your notice, your father does not hold me in the highest opinion, Miss Lavender. I feel sure he would think I wrote the letters myself."

"Oh, I wouldn't say he doesn't respect you. He knows you've uncovered other murderers now. He sees through your act of the carefree dandy."

"I was not speaking of my mental abilities. Rather, I believe your father judges my character to be inferior to the one who would hold claim to your attention."

"And who says you've claimed my attention, Mr. Brummell?"

"I beg your pardon."

Dash it.

"So what are we to do now?"

"First I would like to inspect the physician, Doctor Trusdale's, quarters. I believe he lives above his office."

Miss Lavender looked puzzled. "Why do you think that might help?"

"I wish I could make some intelligent comment on why I want to see his quarters, but the truth is, I merely have a notion there is something in his rooms I should see. Searching other people's property has proven beneficial."

"Do you consider him to be our chief suspect? What of Mrs. Hargrove?"

"Trust me, I have not ruled out the Jacombe housekeeper. Both she and Doctor Trusdale had plenty of motive to kill the man. But stay, I have just had an idea," I said, leaning forward in my chair.

"What?"

"As you said a few minutes ago, the killer has shown remorse for his or her actions. What if we could pit our suspects against one another."

"You mean get them together at the Jacombe residence and accuse one of them?"

"Exactly."

"But what makes you think he or she will confess? The killer has sent you those notes but has allowed Lieutenant Nevill—and Molly—to languish in prison without coming forward. Here we are on the eve of the trial and still there is silence."

"Think of it, though. If we could get the doctor to visit Mrs. Jacombe, and that should not be difficult, we would have him and Mrs. Hargrove together in the presence of the murdered man's wife. Both people are dear to Mrs. Jacombe. If we were to accuse Mrs. Hargrove, and Doctor Trusdale proves to be the killer, he might very well speak up. If we were to accuse the doctor, and Mrs. Hargrove is the killer, it might be enough for her to break down."

"Your scheme might work. We've no other plan, so it will have to do. But which one of them are we going to accuse?"

"We will have to consider the matter carefully. That is another reason for going to the doctor's residence. We shall see if there is any clue there."

Just then, we heard the sound of the back door open, closely followed by raised feminine voices. Molly had come home, and the girls were greeting her.

Miss Lavender and I entered the kitchen in time to see the girl receiving hugs all around. Miss Lavender rushed forward to embrace Molly.

"Oh, but you mustn't touch me," Molly protested. "I need a bath after being in that awful place."

The other girls hurried to make preparations while Miss Lavender, Molly, Lionel, and I stood huddled together.

Molly said, "What are we to do about Nicky? I have worried myself to flinders over him. Tomorrow is the trial!"

"We are still working on the case, Molly," I soothed.

"But time is running out! The word around the prison is that they are sure to convict Nicky because of his stupid confession, and then they'll waste no time in hanging him."

"We have two suspects and a plan," I told her. Then I turned to Lionel. "Lion, run over to Chandos Street and see if there are any lights on in number ten. That is where Doctor Trusdale has his office. I want to search his quarters."

"Right. I'll be back as fast as I can," the boy said and raced out the back door.

"Pray God all is dark and we can get in," Miss Lavender said.

Molly began to cry. "You must find something tonight," she said between sobs. "You must."

32

Lionel soon returned with the news that all was dark at Doctor Trusdale's. "It don't look as if anybody is there. No lights inside anywhere. Even in daylight, the place would need a light or two."

"Excellent. Thank you, Lionel. I shall hurry over right now."

"I'll come with you," Miss Lavender said.

"You most certainly will not," I said. "I am walking a fine line where your father is concerned. It is bad enough he knows we are working together on this case. I shudder to think what he would do to me if he found out you were breaking into people's rooms with me."

"I don't like being left out of things," Miss Lavender replied with a stubborn set to her delicate jaw.

"You will not be. Meet me at my house in two hours' time. We shall go to the Jacombe residence together, to the devil with the conventions. Hopefully, Doctor Trusdale is there. He seems to live in Mrs. Jacombe's pocket."

"How will you account for my presence? You remember the reception I received from members of Society at the Perrys'."

"I shall say you are Miss Lydia Lavender of the Lincolnshire Lavenders. I would have employed such a ruse the other night, but the Perrys already knew who you were."

"All right," Miss Lavender said reluctantly.

I left the shelter at about six of the clock. I took a hackney-coach to save time and lessen the chance of the physician returning while I was in his office.

I had not counted on finding Winston, Doctor Trusdale's assistant, opening the door to the building just as I arrived.

My mind scrambled to find a reason why I was there at that hour, but then I noticed the young man's face. He looked as panicked as I felt. I assumed a superiour tone.

"What are you doing here, Winston? I have an appointment with Doctor Trusdale. We are to have a private consultation. He assured me no one would be about."

"I forgot something, that's all."

Covering for his own error. How fortuitous for me. "Well, open the door and let us in. You can retrieve whatever it is and then leave."

He looked uncertain. "Doctor Trusdale doesn't like anyone left alone here. I'd better stay until he returns."

I assumed my haughtiest demeanor. "Do you know who I am?"

He gulped. "Yes, sir."

"Then do as I say."

He opened the door and scrambled over to his desk behind the counter. I sat in a chair in the waiting area, confident that he would obey me.

And I was right. With only a few more words of protest, and a glance up the stairs, Winston left.

Amazing, is it not, that if one simply assumes control, others will follow with little or no questioning.

I waited a decent five minutes or so before slipping up the stairs. Here I was immediately confronted with a locked door.

Despite daylight outside, the stairway and the door area were dimly lit. I pulled out my pocket knife and set to work on the lock. After a few minutes, I had the door open. I must admit I congratulated myself on my handiwork. Surely a career in lock-picking could be mine should I wish it, do you not agree?

The door opened into a rather large sitting area decorated with more taste than I would have given Doctor Trusdale credit for. Some fine paintings graced the walls. A mahogany upholstered settee, done in dark blue, stood next to a lovely revolving library table with several leather-bound volumes on its smooth surface.

I took a few minutes opening drawers and studying the contents of a personal desk in one corner of the room. This contained nothing more interesting than Doctor Trusdale's tailor's bill. I am always fascinated by what others pay for their clothes, you know.

At any rate, I soon moved into the bedchamber. Here, a curtained bed with a silk valance dominated the smaller room.

My attention was caught by a tiny red candleholder with a small votive lit inside. The light rested on a walnut dressing-table beside a tall window, whose draperies had been shut tight.

I crossed the room swiftly and looked down, amazed by

what I saw. The top of the dressing-table was a shrine of sorts to Mrs. Venetia Jacombe.

A miniature of her nestled in folds of gold velvet at the place of prominence. A small silver container revealed a lock of brown hair tied with a piece of silken string. A stack of folded papers revealed themselves to be notes from Mrs. Jacombe.

There was nothing of a romantic nature in them, only requests for his attention or thanks for services he had performed for her. A few faded party invitations, and a handkerchief with Mrs. Jacombe's initials in one corner, were among the other items.

Here, surely, was proof of an obsessional love on the physician's part for Mrs. Jacombe. A man driven by such passion would very likely kill for the object of his affections.

I thought of all the years that Doctor Trusdale had attended Mrs. Jacombe and harboured this affection for her. The duel between Mr. Jacombe and the innocent young soldier must have been the catalyst that drove Doctor Trusdale to finally have the loathsome Mr. Jacombe out of the way.

I could imagine him going to Vauxhall Pleasure Gardens that night and luring Mr. Jacombe behind the Cascade. Perhaps the note Mr. Jacombe received while at supper was one from the physician, purportedly wishing to give disturbing news about Mrs. Jacombe's health in private. That would explain Mr. Jacombe's willingness to go to the darkened area alone.

I thought of the letters I had received from the killer, the handwriting a good match for that of Doctor Trusdale. Guilt, stemming from the fact that he had taken an oath to save lives, then had taken one himself, propelled him to write to me.

Yes, it all fit. Doctor Trusdale had killed Mr. Jacombe out of a love for the man's wife.

And tonight I would force him to confess.

❧ 33 ❧

Just to be sure that Doctor Trusdale would be at the Jacombe residence that evening, I left a note wedged in the front door telling him that there was urgent news and to please meet me there.

I returned home to Bruton Street to change clothing for the evening and to meet Miss Lavender.

I wish I could report that all was quiet on the Brummell domestic front, but alas, I cannot.

When I walked in the door, it was to find André and Robinson quarrelling with Ned and Ted. Mrs. Ed's cooking was the topic.

At my entrance, André swung toward me. "Monsieur Brummell, have I at any time given you the displeasure?" he asked in his heavy French accent.

"No," I replied.

"Aha! You see," he threw in Ned and Ted's direction. "Monsieur Brummell likes my sauces. This talk of plain, boiled food is sacrilege! From now on, Mrs. Ed cannot come to André's kitchen!"

Ned and Ted immediately jumped to their mother's defense, prompting André to raise his voice again.

"Quiet!" I commanded.

All eyes turned to me.

"I shall not have this disruption in my household. André, you are an excellent chef. Do not change anything of what you are doing. Ned and Ted, your mother's cooking is fine in its own way, but André is right. The kitchen is his domain. Robinson, come upstairs and help me dress for the evening."

A grumbling of voices continued as I ascended the stairs, but I paid no attention. Upon reaching the door to my bedchamber, the sounds of Mrs. Ed singing offkey—to Winifred, the piglet, no doubt—up in the attics assaulted my ears.

I opened the door to the bedchamber and saw Chakkri lying on the bed. Seeing me, the cat flung one brown velvet paw over his eyes.

"Dash it, not that performance again. What is wrong with you, Chakkri? Is it the piglet? Oh, never mind, I must dress. Robinson, fetch some warm water so I might refresh myself."

"Yes, sir."

I walked to the wardrobe. "Let us see, Chakkri. Or no, you do not wish to see, do you? I was about to ask you to help me select an appropriate coat. One to wear to confront a killer, but you remain with one paw covering your eyes."

I suddenly stopped, gazing blankly at my coats. "What was I about, thinking you would help me? This case has made my wits go begging. Hmmm. I think the gentian-blue will be the thing. As for a waistcoat, this figured white one will be just the thing. Ah, Robinson, there you are. I shall need a shave, as well."

For the next half hour I prepared for the evening, filling Robinson in on events in the Jacombe murder case, until it was time to create my cravat. That took my full attention and an extra quarter of an hour, because two of the lengths of linen were not starched properly.

"Mrs. Ed does not approve of starch, you know," Robinson said, trying to bait me.

"Enough. I have a murder investigation that might close this evening if all goes as planned. I count on you to see to the domestic aspects of this household, Robinson."

"Yes, sir. Though I do wish my powers extended to having Mrs. Ed return to Dorset."

"How is the piglet?"

"Mrs. Ed says there has been no improvement in the rash, though the animal eats as though it were healthy as a horse."

"Well then, there is nothing to be worried about. Now Robinson, Miss Lavender will be here at any minute."

Robinson's lips pursed.

"I want you to show her every courtesy, mind you."

"When have I ever not done so, sir?"

A knocking on the front door saved me from answering. Making a final adjustment to my cravat, which rose from my white figured waistcoat like a meringue, I followed Robinson down the stairs.

But it was not Miss Lavender who was revealed when Robinson opened the door. Instead, Mrs. Roucliffe, in all the glory of a blood-red evening gown, stood in the portal. Her face was covered in white lead paint, and she had been liberal in the use of pink tinting on her cheeks and lamp-black on her eyelashes.

Robinson stood at his most contemptuous. "May I help you, madam?"

"Beau, there you are," she said, perceiving me. She swept past Robinson as if he did not exist, securing a place in Robinson's black book forever.

"Good evening, Mrs. Roucliffe. This is a surprise. I am afraid you find me on the point of going out."

"That's all right. I won't stay but a minute. Have you heard the news about Angelica—or Arabella, I should say."

"I do know she killed Mr. Nevill."

"I believe her only to have been defending herself, but still, to know someone who has killed another. Quite shocking."

"Indeed."

"I came to return your handkerchief," she said, pulling that cleaned article from her reticule. "Now, if only that nasty business with Mr. Jacombe's murderer would be cleared up. I can't think for a moment that good-looking young lieutenant had anything to do with it. Though it's just as well someone did away with nasty Mr. Jacombe. I tried to warn his wife about him, you know, but—"

She was interrupted by the arrival of Miss Lavender, who saw me with Mrs. Roucliffe, the latter lady handing me my handkerchief and leaning toward me and confiding in me in a most personal way.

Devil take it.

Mrs. Roucliffe raised one penciled eyebrow at Miss Lavender. "Who is this, Beau?"

Miss Lavender bristled.

I stood speechless for a moment—was it really proper to

introduce Miss Lavender to a member of the demimonde?—
then found my tongue.

"This is Miss Lavender," I said. "Miss Lavender, Mrs.
Roucliffe."

The two women nodded at one another, Mrs. Roucliffe
inclining her head merely an inch.

I took control. "Mrs. Roucliffe, I am certain you will excuse me."

The courtesan straightened her shoulders. "Call on me,
Beau. You know I always like to see you in my house."

She swept out of the hall after making this lethal statement.

Miss Lavender stood like a statue. She wore an emerald-
green-coloured net material with chenille edging over a
light green silk gown. The sleeves were short and gathered
into a narrow, tight band. Her glorious dark red hair was
curled and framed her face.

"Miss Lavender, you look breathtakingly beautiful this
evening," I said.

"Thank you."

I tried again. "She was only here to return a handkerchief
and talk about Arabella. Nothing more."

"You do not have to explain to me."

I thought I did. I wanted to continue to hold Miss
Lavender's confidence, and I knew how hard it was for her
to have given me her trust. "I feel inclined to explain so that
there is no misunderstanding."

"Very well," she said and finally smiled.

"Come now, let us see if together we can catch a killer."

34

The butler answered the door at the Jacombe house, and informed me Mrs. Jacombe was not receiving. I asked to see Mrs. Hargrove instead.

The efficient housekeeper, dressed neatly in another somber black gown, entered the hall. "I am sorry, Mr. Brummell, but Mrs. Jacombe cannot have visitors. Her condition has worsened, and Doctor Trusdale has had to resort to more laudanum to calm her nerves."

"Then the physician is with her?"

"Yes."

"Mrs. Hargrove," I continued, "it is imperative that I see not only Mrs. Jacombe, but you and Doctor Trusdale. I have news regarding Mr. Jacombe's murder and must share it with all of you."

"It will have to wait. I have my orders," Mrs. Hargrove insisted in her calm way.

Frustrated, I asked to see Freddie, realising only at the

last moment that her Royal Highness, the Duchess of York, and Miss Lavender had never met.

We waited in the hall for a few minutes until Freddie, clad in a pale yellow gown, came downstairs.

"George, how delighted I am to see you," she said and looked inquiringly at Miss Lavender.

"Your Royal Highness, may I present Miss Lydia Lavender?"

Miss Lavender dropped into a curtsey.

"You must be John Lavender's daughter," Freddie said.

"Yes, your Royal Highness, I am," Miss Lavender said in surprise.

So much for Miss Lavender of the Lincolnshire Lavenders.

"I am pleased to meet you. George, Mrs. Hargrove tells me you wish to see Lady Venetia. I tell you she is not well."

"I understand. But this is critical. Can she not be moved into the drawing-room for a short time? I must have everyone gathered together to deliver some news."

Freddie considered this a moment. "If you feel this strongly about it, I shall see what I can do. You and Miss Lavender can wait here or in the green sitting-room."

"We shall be fine right here, your Royal Highness. Do try to convince her. The physician, as well."

"Very well."

Freddie disappeared up the stairs, and Miss Lavender turned to me. "The Royal Duchess is a beautiful woman."

"She is, and she does quite a bit of charity work in her county. She has been staying with Mrs. Jacombe since Mr. Jacombe's death, trying to console her on her loss."

There followed an awkward silence. I supposed that Miss Lavender wondered at my relationship with Freddie. I know she had in previous cases. Or perhaps she was just going over in her mind what would happen if we could not assemble the company. I confess once again that the workings of the female mind are mostly a mystery to me.

Thankfully, Mrs. Hargrove reappeared a few minutes later and said that Mrs. Jacombe had agreed to see us in the blue drawing room.

We followed her up the stairs. My brain worked furiously over the plan I had come up with on the way over. So much was at stake.

We entered the drawing-room, and I introduced Miss Lavender. I did not mention that she was John Lavender's daughter. The less said on that score, the better.

Mrs. Jacombe was indeed paler than I had ever seen her. The lady's brown eyes seemed huge in her face, and they were glassy-looking from the laudanum, I surmised. She reclined on the blue-and-silver-striped sofa, the greyhound at her feet.

Freddie sat in the chair closest to her friend.

Doctor Trusdale, who had risen at our entrance, was on the other side of Mrs. Jacombe.

Mrs. Hargrove, knowing that I wished her to remain, had pulled other chairs over so that everyone could be together.

At Mrs. Jacombe's invitation, we all sat down, and I began. "Mrs. Jacombe, it is kind, indeed, of you to see me and Miss Lavender. I assure you I would not have asked you to come from your bed if it were not important."

Doctor Trusdale glared at me and hovered near his patient.

"That is all right, Mr. Brummell," Mrs. Jacombe said in a sad voice. "What news have you?"

"First, I thought you would want to know that the killer

of Mr. Elsworth Nevill has been apprehended. It turns out his daughter-in-law, Arabella Nevill, shot him during an argument between the two."

"Oh dear," she said.

"The good news is that Bow Street has released Molly, Lieutenant Nevill's betrothed, from prison," I said, taking in the look on Mrs. Hargrove's face. She remained as impassive as ever.

"But what of the lieutenant?" Freddie asked. "Have they found out who really killed Mr. Jacombe?"

All eyes were on me. Including the physician's.

"I am afraid that the person who killed Mr. Jacombe is sitting in this room as we speak," I said.

Mrs. Jacombe let out a little cry. The doctor handed her a glass of wine.

"Mr. Brummell," Doctor Trusdale said, "if you have come here to make wild accusations, I shall have to advise Mrs. Jacombe to return to her bed immediately."

"Why, I have not accused anyone yet, Doctor Trusdale," I said, raising my right eyebrow. "But I will now. It is time all the secrets came out, would not you say so, Mrs. Hargrove?"

"I do not know what you mean," the housekeeper said. She looked at Mrs. Jacombe and then back to me. "I agree with Doctor Trusdale that Mrs. Jacombe should not be further upset."

I fixed my gaze on the housekeeper. "Then in that case, perhaps you would like to confess to pulling the trigger right now and spare her any more pain."

Silence fell over the room.

The doctor broke it. "Are you saying that Mrs. Hargrove killed Mr. Jacombe? Your brainbox has suffered a trauma which has left you deficient in reasoning, Mr. Brummell!" Mrs. Jacombe moaned.

"Has it, Doctor Trusdale? But then, you would defend Mrs. Hargrove, would you not? After all, I would be willing to wager that it was you who delivered Mrs. Hargrove's baby all those years ago. You kept the secret of who the baby's father was, too."

"That is enough," Mrs. Hargrove said hotly, showing her temper for the very first time. "I was right here the night Mr. Jacombe was killed, right here in this house. You cannot possibly have any evidence to the contrary."

Mrs. Jacombe looked at me. "Mrs. Hargrove is a trusted servant, Mr. Brummell. You are mistaken."

"Am I? I feel you should know the baby's father—"

"Quiet!" Doctor Trusdale commanded. He stood directly behind where Mrs. Jacombe reclined on the sofa. His eyes shot fire at me. He clearly did not want Mrs. Jacombe to know that her husband had sired Mrs. Hargrove's child.

I stood up so the physician and I would be on equal footing. It seemed my plan was working. "If you do not wish me to continue on in the same vein, Doctor Trusdale, then perhaps you would like to tell us where you were the night Mr. Jacombe was killed."

"Oh, please, do not go on," Mrs. Jacombe begged.

The physician's stern features told me how much he hated me at that moment. Our gazes locked. "I was at home, above my office."

"Do you have any witnesses to corroborate your story?"

"It is not a story, it is the truth."

"Is it? I rather think not. I think you were at Vauxhall Pleasure Gardens that night. I think you had plenty of reasons to want to see Mr. Jacombe dead."

Mrs. Jacombe gasped.

"George," Freddie said. "Is this necessary?"

"Yes, it is necessary, your Royal Highness. A young man has falsely confessed to a crime he did not commit. Tomorrow he will be held accountable during a trial. A trial in which he will most certainly be sentenced to hang. By this time on Saturday, he will be dead." I turned back to the doctor. "Do you want his blood on your hands as well as Mr. Jacombe's?"

"Stop this! Stop it, please!" Mrs. Jacombe cried. Her brown eyes reflected her frenzy. "Doctor Trusdale would have no reason to kill my husband. None."

"On the contrary. He had the most powerful reason of all. Love." I reached into my pocket and pulled out the silver box that contained the lock of Mrs. Jacombe's hair.

Never taking my eyes from Doctor Trusdale, I held it high for the company to see. "Do you care to tell us why you keep this, Doctor Trusdale?"

His face a mask of fury, the doctor said, "How did you get that?"

"Is it really important how I got it? Tell us," I said, opening the box and pulling out the lock of hair, "whose hair is this you keep?"

Doctor Trusdale darted around the sofa to stand in front of me. "Give me that this instant."

"Not until you have answered the question."

Doctor Trusdale lunged forward and grabbed the hair from my hands. He thrust it into his pocket. "I think you must leave now, Mr. Brummell."

"You love Mrs. Jacombe. That is her hair," I said.

"Get out," the physician repeated.

"You love her so much you could not stand to see how her husband treated her."

"Leave before I summon a constable!"

"You knew that with him out of the way you might finally have a chance to make her yours after all these years. What has it been—eighteen, nineteen years since you first fell in love with her?"

"You are mad!" Doctor Trusdale yelled.

"You have a shrine to her in your room, her hair, her miniature, her letters."

"I shall have you arrested," the doctor's voice was shrill.

"You love her so much you went to Vauxhall that night. You sent a note to Mr. Jacombe saying that you must speak to him privately about his wife's condition. When he walked around the back of the Cascade to meet you, you pulled out a pistol and shot him dead."

"No!" screamed Mrs. Jacombe.

She sat bolt upright on the sofa, her chest heaving as if she had been running.

Doctor Trusdale rushed to her side. "Venetia—"

"No more, Doctor Trusdale! I will not have any more of this," Mrs. Jacombe said. "No more lying."

"Venetia, please!" the doctor beseeched.

The invalid's voice was suddenly as strong as iron. "I killed my husband," Mrs. Jacombe said.

Everyone stared at her.

"I killed him because I found out I had been living with a man I did not know for eighteen years. I had been blind."

"Venetia, hush now, I shall send these people away. You need rest. You do not know what you are saying," Doctor Trusdale pleaded.

Mrs. Jacombe shook her head. "No, it is time for you to

stop protecting me. You wrote the letters to Mr. Brummell
for me, and I know it must have been a terrible burden for
you these last ten days, knowing what I have done. But it
is time now for the truth. If only that poor soldier had not
picked up the pistol. I should never have dropped it like
that."

I could not believe my ears.

Miss Lavender's face had drained of all colour.

Freddie sat open-mouthed.

Mrs. Jacombe looked at us all. "You see, all these years,
I thought my husband was a good man. Oh, there were little
indications here and there that he was not perfect. But what
man is? I depended upon him, you know. I have never been
strong enough, and he let me believe that I could not go on
without him. That he took the best of care of me and was
a loyal, loving husband. Then, the day before the Vauxhall
gala, it was a Sunday, I remember, I went walking in Hyde
Park. Doctor Trusdale has always said the fresh air is beneficial."

I nodded. "Go on," I said gently.

"A woman approached me. Mrs. Roucliffe was her name.
She told me how Theobald had tried to set her up as his
mistress. At first, I refused to believe her, but she described
him physically with such accuracy that I had no choice but
to believe that she had lain with him. After that, I started
wondering about a lot of things. His staunch support of Mrs.
Hargrove when she became pregnant. The baby was his, was
it not, Mrs. Hargrove?"

"Yes," the housekeeper replied in a soft voice.

"I thought so. There were others, I have no doubt."

If I could have moved at that moment, I would have stood

next to Miss Lavender, but Mrs. Jacombe's words held me fixed in my place.

"I had been living the proverbial lie for all these years, not seeing the truth that was right in front of me. God only knows what else Theobald was guilty of."

Plenty, I thought.

"When I heard about the duel, I knew Theobald probably had been cheating at cards and would kill that young man. Somehow my husband would manage to come out of it with his reputation intact. He had a marvelous talent for making people believe he was the epitome of the honest man, a man to respect and honour. It was all too clear to me now and too much for me to bear. I could not let him kill that boy. I slipped out of the house that night without even Mrs. Hargrove knowing. Heavily veiled, I went and found a boy to deliver a note to Theobald. In it, I told him I had followed him to the Pleasure Gardens and must speak with him immediately. I never even stopped to think he might tell someone his wife was there. I was out of my mind with humiliation, shame, and anger. As soon as he got close enough to me, I only uttered one word, 'Liar,' before I shot him dead."

"Oh, God, Venetia," Doctor Trusdale groaned.

"I would have come forward before, truly, but I had not the courage. I am glad you came here tonight, Mr. Brummell. I am sorry you had to."

So was I, I thought sadly.

❧ 35 ❧

Friday afternoon, I stood in the kitchen at the Haven
of Hope, the remnants of a small celebration around me.
Molly had spent the morning making cakes, and the other
girls helped prepare a sumptuous repast for Lieutenant Nevill to enjoy his first day out of prison.

He sat back in his chair, positioned close to Molly. The
two had eyes only for each other.

"What will you do now?" Miss Lavender asked the lieutenant.

"Molly and I shall marry as soon as possible. With the
money Grandfather left me, we can purchase a place in the
country. Neither of us finds Town life appealing."

"The country!" Lionel exclaimed. "Who'd want to live
there when they could live in London?"

Miss Lavender smiled at the boy.

"You plan to give up your position in the army then?" I
asked Lieutenant Nevill.

"Yes. Molly and I want a large family. A soldier's life would hardly be suited to that."

"Nicky and I will be quite content being a country couple," Molly said.

I was happy for them. The lieutenant had finally been released that morning after Mrs. Jacombe came forward. Though I was very happy the lieutenant was free, I could not help but feel sorry for Mrs. Jacombe.

Mr. Lavender stood on the fringe of the gathering, feeling a bit guilty, I expect. I walked over to him.

"What will happen to Mrs. Jacombe?" I asked.

He rolled a toothpick around in between his lips. "They'll be sympathetic. She'll likely be judged insane. That physician friend of hers will see that she gets humane treatment."

"No common madhouse then?"

"I doubt it. She has money and position. A private institution, I expect."

Miss Lavender walked over to join us. "The two of you are not arguing, are you?"

I smiled. "No, our conversation has been quite civil."

The Bow Street man looked at me askance. "I'm waiting for you to say you told me I had the wrong man in gaol."

"Oh, now, when have you ever known me to gloat?"

Mr. Lavender snorted.

The party was breaking up. I wanted to see Miss Lavender alone. "Miss Lavender, the day is very fine. I wonder if you might walk with me by the Serpentine."

"Lydia has to help the girls clean up," Mr. Lavender said, scowling at me.

An imp of mischief appeared in Miss Lavender's green eyes. "Actually, I think just this once I'll let the girls handle things themselves. The day is fine, as Mr. Brummell said."

Under her father's disapproving eye, I hailed a hackney-coach to take us to Hyde Park. Miss Lavender wore a pretty rose-coloured gown which, oddly enough, only complimented her dark red hair.

When we arrived at the Park, we strolled amiably in silence until we reached the waters of the Serpentine. I felt good just having her hand tucked in the crook of my arm.

We came to a place at the water's edge and stopped. A light breeze came across the water, rustling Miss Lavender's curls.

"Are you glad it is all over?" I asked in a low voice.

"Of course."

"Is it *all* over?" I asked, turning to look into her eyes. I knew she realised I meant her feelings about Mr. Jacombe.

She looked down for a moment, the toe of her shoe scuffing the ground. It seemed an eternity until she looked back into my eyes. "Yes, I think it is."

I reached into my pocket and withdrew a small jewellery box. Suddenly, I felt like a boy of six-and-ten summers. "Here, I, er, got this for you."

Miss Lavender looked at me in some surprise. "You bought me a present?"

"Well, I, ahem. 'Present' is a strong word, eh? Why not open it, and perchance you will see why I thought of you when I saw it."

She opened the box. The gold heart lay nestled in white satin. "Oh, how perfectly lovely," she said, her lips curving.

"I thought, that is, with everything dreadful you have been through, that, well, that . . ." For once my well-known cool composure failed me.

"Yes, Mr. Brummell, I believe I know what you mean. I have felt these past days that the weight of the years and my horrid experience with Mr. Jacombe has slowly begun to lift from my shoulders."

"That is all for the best."

She reached up and touched the gold chain around her neck. The one that contained the key to the box with the scraps of that dress. The one she had worn since Mr. Jacombe had so cruelly taken her innocence.

"Will you hold this for me for a moment?" Miss Lavender said, handing me the box containing the gold heart.

"Of course."

Miss Lavender raised her hands slowly and removed the chain with the key from about her neck. "I've worn this for almost seven years," she said.

She looked at the silver key for a long moment, then with a fluid movement, she flung the key on its necklace high into the air and above the river. It glinted in the sunlight before it fell with a tiny splash into the water.

Miss Lavender looked at me, her eyes suspiciously bright. I hoped she would not cry. Crying females are not my specialty, you must know.

Thankfully, she merely asked if I would help her put on the new necklace with the heart. There followed a bit of fumbling on my part, as my fingers touched the warm skin of Miss Lavender's neck while I fastened the clasp.

When I was done, she reached up and touched the gold heart. "I know it looks lovely, even though I don't have a glass to see."

"I assure you, it is even more lovely now, lying against your skin."

She smiled then and slipped her hand into mine.

•   •   •

Later that night, I was feeling quite relaxed as Robinson helped me prepare for bed.

"So Mrs. Ed departed this afternoon?" I inquired.

"Yes, sir. She said Winifred the piglet's rash must be a *London* rash, and she must return to the country."

"Ned and Ted must be sorry she left."

"Yes," Robinson replied with a hint of a smile.

Chakkri chose that moment to spring silently onto the coverlet. "Ah, Chakkri, nice of you to grace me with your presence," I said.

"Reow."

Robinson's lips pursed.

I noted that Chakkri stared at me with his deep blue eyes and waited to be petted.

"I see you are not covering your eyes any longer, Chakkri. Had you noticed the odd mannerism, Robinson?"

"No, sir, I cannot say I was blessed with that knowledge."

"I expect you were blind to it, then. You may go now, Robinson. I wish you a good-night."

With that, I blew out the candle at my bedside, only Chakkri's rumbling purrs disturbing the peaceful night.